MW01074761

AND THE DEVIL CRIED

KRISTOPHER TRIANA

STYGIAN SKY MEDIA

STYGIAN SKY MEDIA

Houston, Texas
www.stygianskymedia.com/

Copyright © 2021 Kristopher Triana

All Rights Reserved

ISBN: 978-1-63951-000-9

First Edition

The story included in this publication is a work of fiction. Names, characters, places and incidents are products of the author's imagination or are used fictitiously. Any resemblance to actual events or locales or persons living or dead is entirely coincidental.

Without limiting the rights under copyright reserved above, no part of this publication may be reproduced, stored in or introduced into a retrieval system, or transmitted, in any form, or by any means (electronic, mechanical, photocopying, recording, or otherwise), without the prior written permission of both the copyright owner and the above publisher of this book.

Cover Art: Alex McVey

Book Layout: Lori Michelle
www.TheAuthorsAlley.com

for Ryan Harding

you're as bad as me

"Happy shall he be, that taketh and dasheth thy little ones against the stones."

Psalm 137:9

PROLOGUE

LET ME TELL you about the man I killed.

His name was Dennis Kingsley, a fifty-nine-year-old widower with two grown children, who lived alone in a modest house in Norwich.

Of course, I didn't know any of this until after I'd murdered him.

To me he was just a stranger who'd cleaned up at the craps table in Foxwoods, a resort casino owned by the Mashantucket Indian tribe. I'd been standing at the table as long as he had when I got down to my last twenty-five-dollar chip, the minimum bet. I decided to play the field because it seemed to have good odds. I was not an experienced gambler and didn't understand what a sucker bet this actually was—how it only gives the player the illusion it's a good bet by making them believe they have more ways to win than lose.

But Kingsley knew sucker bets from solid ones. He was absolutely slaughtering the table. And if I'd been wise, I would have bet alongside him as so many others were. Instead my last chip was lost as he rolled lucky number seven. Meanwhile, Kingsley had stacks of hundred-dollar chips lined up before him like some kind of Checkers champion.

1

Once my buddy Nick lost enough, we decided to play the slots with what quarters we had left, mostly so we could at least score some free drinks to compensate for our financial losses.

"You believe that old bastard?" Nick asked, pulling the lever of his machine. "He was killing it. I'll bet he won three grand tonight just at that table alone."

I grimaced. "Lucky prick."

An evil heat moved up through my sternum, the familiar hellfire of envy. Unlike Nick, I hadn't come here just for a good time. I'd been desperate to turn my meager savings of five hundred dollars into something substantial enough to fund an escape. My girlfriend and I wanted to get a place together and it was never going to happen without enough cash for the first and last month's deposit on the apartment we'd been looking at. Now, in less than two hours, I'd lost my entire nest egg. She would be crestfallen, but her unhappiness wasn't what stressed me most. I was so sick of where I lived it made my blood burn. The indignation must have shown on my face because Nick patted my shoulder, but before he could say a consoling word I shoved his hand off.

His smile disappeared. "Take it easy, man."

"You take it easy. I'm fuckin' broke. Goddamned Indians."

Ken and Tina rejoined us, red-eyed and giggly from the joint they'd smoked outside. She'd stolen his Bruins baseball cap and was hanging on him like a purse. He managed to flag down a waitress. Everyone asked for beers while I ordered a belt of bourbon. She carded us and I gave her my brother's driver's license.

We looked enough alike, especially now that I'd grown my hair out. The waitress wiggled away to fetch our drinks.

Hard liquor would either mellow me out or increase my anger. I could never predict which.

As we drank, the others talked about the same uninteresting, unimportant bullshit as everyone else our age. I'd heard all this inane chatter countless times before, but tonight every word seemed to fill my mind with corrosive acid. I ground the ice from my drink into my teeth, the pain a welcome distraction from the company of these people.

Dennis Kingsley walked through the row of slot machines just beside ours. Nick didn't notice—too busy sneaking a glance at Tina's ample cleavage—but I watched the old fuck carry his chips past, a crooked smile on his prune face. He had so many he needed a tray to carry them to the cash-out counter.

I stood. "I'm taking off."

"Dude," Ken said. He gave me a curious look. "We've only been here for, like, three hours."

"Less than that," Nick said, almost pained.

I shrugged. "Yeah, well a casino ain't no fun when you've got no money."

"It's a long drive home," Tina said.

"Fuck it."

Kingsley approached the cashier's window. My friends tried to talk me into staying, extolling the virtues of the band that would play later. We'd planned this trip for weeks and had come up from Long Island, almost a hundred miles south of here. But I'd never given a fuck about having a good time with them. That's why I'd driven myself instead of joining the others in Tina's car. I was here solely for the cash, and all I'd done was lose it.

I grabbed my jacket off the stool beside me. Tina took my arm.

"C'mon, Jack," she whined. "Don't bail already."

In no mood for her bullshit, I shoved her off even harder than Nick. I've never felt there was a reason to be nice to a girl you've already fucked.

About a month prior she, Ken, and I had gotten high on ecstasy at his house, and they'd asked me to videotape them having sex. Later on, we started on a bottle of vodka. Ken passed out drunk in his bed. Tina and I sat on the floor, taking hits from a skull bong. She was just high and horny enough to be malleable when I made a move on her, and with our clothes half on we fucked quietly on the carpet so not to wake up her boyfriend. The whole thing was over in fifteen minutes and I came inside her without asking if it was okay. Ken had once mentioned to me that Tina was on the pill. She got pissed at me anyway, but what was she going to do? Complain to Ken about it? Her outrage didn't last long though. I often got the sense she wanted to fuck me again—this time without her unconscious boyfriend around, so we could take our time and enjoy it. I figured I could have her again if I wanted to, but wasn't willing to put any effort into the pursuit. She had great tits but a rather plain face, with boney legs and a nonexistent ass. Ken could keep her.

"See ya," I said.

I crushed my plastic cup, tossing it to the floor. From the corner of my eye I could see Nick shaking his head with a slight scowl on is face. I had the urge to turn around and confront him but didn't want to lose sight of Kingsley.

I wasn't even sure what the old prick planned to do. I just figured he would go up to his room and give me an opportunity to roll him. I considered jumping him in the elevator. *No, too many cameras.* The casino was lousy with them—some out in the open, many more hidden in statues of wolves and eagles and other woodland creatures. But there were no cameras inside the hotel rooms themselves. If I followed Kingsley, I might be able to rush him once he unlocked his door. Force him inside, knock him out cold, cash in the chips, bail before the bastard returned to his senses. I'd committed crimes before, just never anything this violent. I wasn't going to let that deter me, though. I wanted that money. I *needed* that money.

Things didn't play out that way.

After Kingsley cashed out, he didn't go to the elevators. Instead he headed to the front exit. A bead of panic-sweat slithered down my spine. The parking lot almost certainly had as many eyes in the sky as the casino. And there were too many people going in and out of the casino at all hours anyway. No chance I could jump him out there.

We exited the building. Kingsley stopped to talk to someone. I lit a cigarette and leaned against a concrete pillar. If these men came together, I'd have to forfeit my effort to rob the old man. I'd already been thinking about quitting the hunt as it was. When Kingsley said goodnight to the guy, however, something within me rejoiced, egging me on, and I pursued him through the parking lot like a shadow.

My car was only four rows away. I could follow him a while, maybe get him at the next place he stopped.

I expected him to be driving something expensive and sporty. A Jaguar or Mercedes maybe. Instead he opened the door of a Hyundai. There was a dealer frame around the license plate: *Sentry Hyundai and Subaru—Norwich, Connecticut.*

Norwich.

Only fifteen minutes away.

Doing my best to look casual, I hurried to my shitty Celica. The rush was unnecessary. Kingsley took his time backing out—typical grandpa. I grimaced, imagining him smugly pawing through a fistful of cash, dentures glistening in a shit-eating grin.

I followed him, keeping what I hoped was a safe distance, figuring only a cop or a criminal would notice being tailed. We made it to where he lived in twelve minutes. A nice neighborhood. Generic. Nothing fancy. It seemed the old guy wasn't as wealthy as I assumed, just had one hell of a good night at the casino.

As he pulled into his driveway, I turned down a side road, circling the neighborhood before parking just down the street, close enough so I could watch the lights in Kingsley's windows. I waited over an hour for them to go out, sitting in my car with the tinted windows up, not even smoking so neighborhood watch types wouldn't know the car was occupied. When at last Kingsley's lights went out, I exited the car, opened the trunk, and retrieved the crowbar I always used for break-ins.

It was a cloudy night that hid the moon. Great for

cover. I'd long ago gotten over the jittery nerves that came with burglaries, but my first break-in with someone home? My heart thundered. I walked around the back of the house to make sure the bedroom lights were off, then sat beneath the shadows of a hemlock tree, waiting. I felt like a dog watching a rabbit through a fence. I checked my watch. After half an hour passed, I worked the crowbar against the rear sliding door's lock, wedging it into the handle. I pulled and shoved, biting my bottom lip. There was little noise, but also little movement. The door wasn't giving at all. Always prone to rage with stubborn inanimate objects, I jammed the crowbar too hard and missed the frame, causing the whole pane to burst.

This changed everything. Stealth no longer an option, all I could do was charge inside. If I were quick, I could still catch the old man off guard. The absence of moonlight made for a blindingly dark living room. I stumbled around, my knee hitting an end table.

The hinges on a door creaked and a beam of light fell through the opening. I spun around just as the shotgun went off.

I felt only a sting on my left side, my arm and ribs growing hot with pinpricks of pain. I charged the gun-wielding shadow. When I got close the shotgun revealed itself to be a double barrel. I had no way to know if Kingsley had fired one or both chambers. Not wanting to take my chances, I went for a blow that could do the most damage, swinging the crowbar at the old man's head. His reflexes were poor, and he didn't come close to getting out of the way. He fell backward into the master bedroom, into the soft, amber glow of the nightstand lamp. The right side of his face was indented, the cheekbone pulverized. Fractured skull or not, the shotgun was still within his reach, so I brought the crowbar down upon his arm, breaking it. I was surprised he remained conscious. I straddled him on the floor, sitting on his chest.

"Where's the money?"

Kingsley began to cry. *Embarrassing*. I spat in his face with disgust.

"Where's the money, asshole?"

He murmured. "Wha . . . what money?"

"The money from the casino!"

His eyes widened. "Who are you? I . . . I don't have any money . . . "

I glowered down at him. The whole situation had been too noisy—shattering glass, gunshots. Neighbors were bound to be dialing 911 *right now*. I grew increasingly impatient, increasingly agitated. My side continued to burn and the sleeve of my coat was punched with tiny tears. The shotgun blast had caused some minor peppering to my skin. I asked Kingsley again about the cash. Patience wearing thin, I punched him in the nose before he could answer.

"Please," he said. "Please . . . in my coat . . . "

He pointed. I stood, grabbed the shotgun, and approached the closet. Inside was the suit he'd worn to Foxwoods. I dug into the pockets, finding a wallet and a slip of paper. The wallet held just forty-two bucks. When I brought the slip of paper to the lamplight, I realized why.

It was a check from Foxwoods, made out to

Kingsley, for just under four grand. To me, it was worthless.

My hands trembled. "Son of a bitch . . . "

I kicked Kingsley in the ribs, then straddled him again and placed the crowbar across his neck. That mean heat flamed through my solar plexus, my eyes wide and unblinking. My hate for the old man was suddenly titanic.

"You miserable fuck!" I said. "Where's your safe?"

Kingsley wheezed. "I don't . . . have a . . . safe."

Scanning the bedroom, I noticed the worn, outdated furniture. A twin bed with pillows stained by head grease. The end table was nicked and scratched and stained. Even the lamp looked like a relic from the '70s. There was a water stain in one corner of the popcorn ceiling and the dust-sheathed blades of an oscillating fan propped up on a chair.

This was no high-rolling gambler—just a lower-middle-class Joe who'd had a lucky night.

But that luck had run out with me.

Holding the crowbar in both hands, I pressed down on his Adam's apple until his face purpled. Honestly, I'd only wanted him to pass out so I would have time for a proper getaway. It wasn't until the following day when I saw Kingsley's house on the news that I learned I'd strangled him to death.

I'd only wanted the guy's money. I'd gotten away with a lousy forty-two bucks and a used shotgun. For that, I'd killed a man.

But hey, what the hell did I know?

I was only seventeen then.

At least I never got caught.

PART ONE

PRETTY IN PINK

CHAPTER ONE

PINO SENT A car for me the day I got out.

The kind gesture was unexpected. Sure beat taking the bus. Pino and I had been in business together in the joint, and even after his release we'd continued a friendly partnership, Pino's outfit supplying me with prescription painkillers to distribute through MacDougall-Walker Correctional Institution—an overly long name for a Level IV security prison. Pino told me to look him up once I was released, but the moment I was a free man he'd been the one to call on me.

The driver of the Lincoln was in a chauffeur's outfit, complete with a cap upon his grayed head. I'd almost expected Pino to be in the back, waiting for me with a bottle of champagne. Instead, all that was on the seat was a flask full of bourbon, a fresh pack of Camels, and a money clip bulging with two grand in twenties.

"Should I go straight to Mr. Lucchese's?" the driver asked.

I nodded and lit a cigarette. For ten cartons of these Camels, I could have someone murdered in prison. I wondered how much an assassin could make on the outside these days. After six years in the joint,

I knew little about price inflation in the so-called civilized world.

As we drove off the government property, a feeling of weightlessness struck me, my freedom intoxicating me even without the whiskey. I could see so much of the early summer sky and the lush green trees were like a stunning virtual reality. We made it to West Hartford in less than half an hour. The town was infinitely nicer than the skanky destitution of Hartford, where poverty-stricken blacks had turned the streets into graffitied crack alleys spattered with cigarette butts and broken glass. As we went through this quaint Connecticut town, I marveled at simple sights. A freshly painted manor house with Bougainvillea in the garden; a Corvette the color of Christmas cherries; train tracks and a trademark New England covered bridge.

Most of all, I noticed the women. It was a warm day in June and they wore light clothing, the younger ones in shirts that showed their bellies and short shorts to rival Daisy Duke. A gaggle of teenagers walked through the shopping district, flipping skateboards and fingering their phones. The girls of the group were only just beginning to blossom. Bee-sting breasts and skinny legs and braces that glittered when they smiled. Two women in their forties were coming out of a Jewish deli. They looked like a couple of yentas with their big hair and heavy jewelry. I admired their thick, generous asses.

A lot of cons told me the longer you're locked away from women the harder it becomes to talk to them.

I wasn't concerned.

We pulled into a circular driveway that led to a

two-story house with a widow's peak and wraparound porch. I stepped out of the car. The grass shimmered in the breeze and I knelt to run my hand through it. Soft as a pussycat. Somewhere the voice of a sports announcer crackled from a television. I heard the joyous calls of children riding bikes down the street. A lawnmower hummed in the distance. When a blue jay flew by, its colors were almost too intense for my eyes. I took a pull on the flask, blinking as if coming out of a dream. My time inside had been concrete-gray, stale and lifeless. To me, the outside world was like fireworks.

The driver pulled the car away. I didn't know if I should tip him—and didn't care either. The world around me was as bright as a cartoon, rich and splendiferous and pulsing with the crisp energy of being alive. I didn't have time to ring the bell before the front door opened.

Standing before me was a girl of about sixteen, her dark hair wet. Clad in a bikini top with a beach towel around her waist, she smelled of chlorine and youth and her chocolate eyes looked me up and down, expressionless. If this weren't Pino Lucchesse's daughter, I might have nailed her right there on the front stoop. After six years of fucking prison trannies up the ass, the urge to take her was enough to make my teeth grind.

The girl didn't ask my name or why I was there.

"Dad!" she called over her shoulder. "It's for you."

She didn't invite me in—the little cunt didn't even say hello—but she let the door swing open, and I stepped inside.

Pino's house wasn't a mansion, but it was far nicer

than any place I'd ever lived. Matching white furniture; futuristic-looking reading lamps; a metallic refrigerator. On the kitchen counter, a stray bag of potato chips lay amongst an assortment of open soda cans—all considered luxuries in the joint. I was about to take my shoes off out of respect for the floors when Pino came bounding into the anteroom in his robe and flip-flops. He wore a gold necklace with a pendant of St. Jude and an assortment of rings I at first mistook for brass knuckles. His skin was deeply tanned and it looked as if he'd had hair implants, the receding hairline now covered by a fine, silvery pompadour.

"Jackie!" he said, arms outstretched over his cauldron-like belly.

I despised hugging but opened my arms to embrace him. He patted my back, his hoarse laughter in my ear.

"How the hell are ya?" he asked, stepping back to get a better look at me.

"I'm free. That says it all."

"Ain't that the truth?"

"You're looking good, Pino. Got that Vegas tan. Look well-fed."

He patted his gut. "I tell ya, the wife's an even better cook than when I went inside." Pino turned his head and yelled. "Rosalie! We got company!"

He led me through the living room to glass doors that opened out to the swimming pool. A woman rose from her lawn chair where she'd been sunbathing. She was younger than Pino, but not by much, maybe mid-forties. She wore a one-piece bathing suit, her stout legs pocked with cellulite. Huge press-on nails.

Enormous sunglasses hid most of her face. She said hello and went right past us to prepare something for me in the kitchen, asking if I wanted something cool like a nice caprese salad.

I said yes just to shut her up and sipped from my flask.

"Don't bother with that rotgut now," Pino told me. "I'll fix us up some of the good stuff."

Fresh drinks in hand, we ventured outside. Pino's daughter sat at a table under an umbrella, texting. Two pre-teen boys fought in the pool with big, foam noodle swords. Pino shouted at them to stop making such a damn racket and guided me toward the table. The closer we got, the more I saw of his daughter. A caramel thigh flashed from under the towel in an alluring peek-a-boo. I sipped my drink to distract myself.

"Drea," Pino said, patting the girl's shoulder. "Give me and my friend here some space."

Drea rose from her seat without taking her eyes off the phone's screen, hips swaying as she walked off.

"Kids," Pino said. He raised his glass. "How's this Blanton's?"

"Sure beats toilet wine."

He let loose a hearty fat guy chuckle. "Ain't that the truth? Everything go smoothly on the way out?"

"An easy transition. Mickey's got everything he needs."

"And you're sure he's the right guy for the job?"

"Like I said before, I know he was low level when you were in there, but he's been my right hand for the past two years now. He doesn't take any shit but still keeps a cool head. Everybody shows him respect. He's good with numbers and details and he's made solid connections with some of the bulls. Mickey's not just the right guy to replace me, he's the only guy who can handle it."

Pino shrugged. "I hear you. But I have other guys inside."

"C'mon. Who you gonna use? Frank? Marty, maybe? They're okay guys but compared to Mickey they're a bunch of chumps."

"Easy there, Jackie. Marty's my cousin."

"No offense intended, Pino. I'm just telling you straight. You don't know how the politics have changed inside. Without Mickey's leadership, the whole drugstore ring is gonna end up back in the hands of the spics."

"God forbid."

Rosalie came out of the house with the salad. The tomato slices and mozzarella made me realize how hungry I actually was, particularly for food that wasn't mess hall slop. I couldn't remember the last time I'd eaten fresh basil. Rosalie asked if we needed anything else and when Pino shooed her away she kissed her husband on the cheek and left.

"All right," he told me. "Enough about Mickey. This is your first day out, let's not talk about the can, huh?" He patted my arm. "You got the cash from the car, right?"

"Yeah. Need me to do something?"

He waved the notion away. "Nah, nah. That's my welcome home gift. Help you back on your feet."

"Thanks, Pino. But I'm ready to work."

"I respect your initiative, Jackie, but you've got to ease into things. I know you from the joint. The other guys? They don't know your ass from Adam. Besides, you wanna keep your parole officer happy by looking clean during your first month. I hear you got stuck with Autry."

"Yeah. You know him?"

"Just things I hear. He's from down south, a real bubba. Not the worst PO you could land but not the easiest either. Don't sweat it, Jackie. I've got a little something set up for ya, to keep him from bustin' balls. But first things first." He drew a cigar from the box on the table a lit up. "Let Pino show you a good time."

We had an early dinner at one of the upscale dago restaurants Pino frequented. Believing I was Italian, he figured I would want a good meal first and foremost. When I'd met Pino in the joint, I'd lied to him and said I was a guinea. It made it easier to get in the man's favor. My real last name didn't end in a vowel, so I'd told him my mother's maiden name was De Feo. And instead of going by Jack, as I always had, I'd introduced myself as Jackie. The name stuck.

For my first dinner as a free man, I ordered eggplant parmesan and barbera at Pino's recommendation. A fine dish, but only a prelude to what I was really hungry for. I watched the olive-skinned hostess as she fluttered about the room. She was young but had already filled out, her black dress barely containing her. Her high heels bore leather straps that rose around her calves like serpents.

Pino caught me staring at her. "She's a nice slice of pie, ain't she? They're great at that age."

I nodded. "I honestly thought we'd be having dinner at a gentlemen's club tonight."

"Patience, Jackie. I know the first thing a guy wants once he gets out is to open a box, but there's no sense eating that strip club food. I tell you, since my release I've learned to savor things. It's important to enjoy all of life's pleasures."

I watched the hostess bend over her podium to write something. "I'm sitting here eating eggplant while that slut should be eating mine."

Pino snickered. "You dirty son of a bitch. *Mangia*—then a woman. I've got it all worked out for you. A friend of mine's in the escort business."

"Some things never change."

"Yeah, well, his girls are a little better looking than yours were."

"Better not let Lexi hear you say that. You'll break her heart."

Pino laughed but didn't reply. Like most prison wolves, he didn't want to talk about the trannies he'd fucked while incarcerated. Homosexuality is common in prison. Even heterosexual guys like Pino took to sodomizing other men. You can't just jerk off for five to ten years; you need the physical touch of another human body, so your best bet is to look for a clean, young man to be your submissive, to play the role of the woman in a sexual relationship. Many newcomers can be easily dominated, but while those virgins are obedient, they're never what you'd call enthusiastic. For that you need a *true* homosexual. The kind of guy who'd want a man even if he weren't locked up.

I was twenty-seven when I began my sentence for armed robbery. It was my first long stint in the joint.

I abstained from sex for months, but then I got a new cellmate. Ginger was a skinny, feminine young man with a ponytail and little body hair. She managed to seduce me one night by begging me to let her suck my cock. After that, I started fucking her regularly. As long as Ginger shaved her ass it was fairly easy to imagine she was a real woman.

Friendly with a group of queens on our block, Ginger introduced me to them to discuss my idea of forming a prostitution ring. Lexi and Star were soon on board with me as their daddy, with Ginger serving as my bottom bitch. Nobody fucked Ginger except me. I fucked Lexi and Star too, of course, but also rented out their mouths and assholes for cigarettes, Ramen Noodles, green dot cards, clean urine, and other forms of prison currency. The only payment the girls received was protection—which they were damn grateful to have after being brutally raped multiple times. The few nice things I did reward them with— lipstick, blush, bras, panties—also benefited our bustling business. Eventually I got them electric shavers to keep their bodies smooth. One time a john tried to steal Lexi's to make a tattoo gun out of its guts, and when I caught him I shoved every broken bit of the shaver up his ass, tearing his rectum and putting him in the infirmary. It didn't take long for the rest of the block to respect me as these queens' pimp, and seeing as they were now my property, I chose to do with them what I wished.

Star was some sort of octoroon. Not a milado, but definitely part black—though not so much as to cause an issue with any of the white supremacists. The problem I *did* have was she had a big dick and tended to get hard when servicing a john. After fielding a number of complaints, I warned Star to stay flaccid while getting fucked so the tape wouldn't come loose. I'm sure she tried but just couldn't control her body's response. The complaints about her giant cock continued, so I made a few businesses deals and had a gang of Puerto Ricans attack her in the showers, castrating her with a knife snuck in by a guard who I paid off with blowjobs from Lexi. Star lost that big dick of hers as well as her balls. After that she was more popular than ever. Seeing an opportunity to improve my product, Lexi was given the same sex change operation. And even though I didn't rent out Ginger I castrated her myself just for my own pleasure. That's when they started calling me The King of Queens. Seeing potential in me, Pino went from a customer to a business partner, and I expanded my operation to include narcotics and other services.

"You got a place to stay?" Pino asked, cutting into his veal.

"No."

"Relatives?"

"None I'd like to visit."

I hadn't talked to my parents in years and was even further estranged from my extended family. It suited me just fine to be their little cross to bear.

"That's what I thought," Pino said, "based on what you'd told me. Like I said, I think I have something that'll work out good for you, but I need to get it all in place tomorrow. For tonight, we'll put you up in a hotel. It's nothing fancy, but irregardless it's a discrete place, one my friend uses for his escorts."

"I really appreciate this, Pino."

I knew he was pulling me in for his own purposes. If he took care of me, I'd become indebted. For now, I allowed myself to be pampered. I wanted to keep working for Pino, at least until I could work for someone bigger.

"I just need to know one thing," Pino said.

"What's that?"

He smiled as he chewed. "Now that we're talking real women, I need to know your type."

The hostess walked by again, leading a family to their table.

"Young," I said.

Pino had downplayed the quality of the inn. It was small and simple, but everything is The Ritz-Carlton once you've called a shared cell with a metal toilet home. Just to lie down on a real bed instead of a skimpy cot was a luxury. I kicked out of my shoes and stripped down to just my slacks and tank top undershirt, one from the package of three I'd been given upon my release along with three pairs of boxers and socks. I opened the curtains to enjoy the second story view. It'd been so long since I'd seen the moon and stars. I didn't even bother turning on the television.

The knock at the door startled me and I wished Pino had given me a rod. I'd asked for one—something simple like a snubnosed revolver. He'd advised against it. Though I'd been released, my freedom felt somehow like stolen goods, as if I were on the run. I felt like any minute I could be swarmed upon by bulls who would haul me back into a cell, citing some overlooked technicality. So while I remembered the escort was coming, I checked the peephole anyway. I told myself the paranoia would fade, that this was just the first baby step in the closing of a great wound.

The girl wasn't as young as I would have liked, but she was no older than thirty with pale skin and blonde hair, as I'd asked, and she wasn't just one of those handjob Orientals but a true sex worker. Her black dress was similar to the one the hostess had worn, only without sleeves. I hadn't asked for any particular outfit. The only clothing I insisted upon was what she wore underneath.

"Take the dress off," I said, before she was even through the door.

"Eager beaver," she said, coyly. "You know I'm dying for you too, baby."

If she hadn't belonged to Pino's friend, I would have backhanded her for this *faux* playfulness. I couldn't stand a woman pretending to like me. She closed the door and I grabbed at the hem of her dress and pulled it up, revealing pink panties with little embroidered strawberries. Though the color was what was important to me, the fruit was a titillating bonus. The hooker moaned as my hands explored her and she did as she was told, pulling the dress over her head.

"Want me to suck it, baby?"

I shoved her onto the bed facedown. I'd had enough of mouths.

CHAPTER TWO

Gɪᴜsᴇᴘᴘᴇ'ꜱ ᴡᴀꜱ ᴀɴ old school deli, the kind that's hard to find outside New York or Jersey. They carried eccentric cold cuts and moldy salamis and made their own roast beef. A worn poster of *The Godfather* hung in a frame by the cash register along with pictures of old boxers and an autographed photo of Dom DeLuise. Stalks of garlic hung from the ceiling like sleeping bats and boxes of S. Pellegrino lined the walls. A stout guinea named Giuseppe Camarata owned the place. He was only fifty but had gone gray with a bald spot on his crown. He only wore white t-shirts, checkered slacks, and an apron, all of which were perpetually stained pink from meat cutting. He had immigrated to the states some thirty years ago and spoke English well, but preferred to work in the back of the house and let other people run the counter. People like me.

Pino set me up with the job as well as an apartment nearby. There were long windows that offered a fair amount of sunlight and a decent view only obstructed by the two-story building for rent across the street, a former Walgreens. The apartment was minimally furnished, which would do until I could start making real money through Pino. To start, however, I needed a straight job. I wasn't high enough on the ladder to just have a timecard punched for me either. I had to actually work at the deli, slicing and packaging cold cuts and tolerating pain in the ass old ladies who could never decide how much they wanted or how thin it should be. I came home at night with aching feet, reeking of those intense dago cheeses. But I did eat well.

One of my coworkers was a natural blonde in her thirties. Natalie Moore was short with an ass that made up for her lack of tits. She wasn't a knockout, but had soft eyes and softer skin, and overall girl-next-door good looks. She wore no ring. With the customers she was very friendly and outgoing, but when working alone with me she fell quiet. This made conversation with a woman all the more difficult for me. The cons who'd warned me about this had been right after all. I second-guessed my every move—too persistent one minute, too genteel the next. I tried sticking to pop culture, but my knowledge was six years outdated. Current events and sports were also lost on me. When I managed to get her to tell me what she was into, she was as bland as dry oatmeal. But I wasn't going to give up on her. For the sake of my pride, I needed to fuck a woman I didn't pay for, and Natalie was currently the only one in my life.

Giuseppe always played traditional rat pack songs or Pavarotti to add to the Italian atmosphere. When he took Sundays off, though, Natalie would plug her phone into the system and play empty pop crap. I pretended to like it. This loosened her up a bit.

"So where're you from?" she asked one Sunday.

I was making some headway. "Port Jeff, originally."

"Long Island?"

"Yeah, north shore. You?"

"Oh, I'm from here. I've always lived here."

I smiled. "In the deli?"

She smiled back. I'd finally opened her.

On my downtime I worked out, trying to maintain my prison-sculpted form even without the weights. I needed more income to join a gym. I visited the library, went to the movies, and took long walks when the sun went down and everything cooled. Most of all I stayed out of the apartment. Being outside was everything to me now.

Once a week I visited Hugh Autry at the parole office. A cold, sterile building for a cold, sterile man. I answered his questions as politely as I could stand to, biting back my attitude. I had to submit to a saliva test each visit, so I couldn't smoke grass or pop OC, but I could do an occasional line of blow as long as it was several days before a check-in. Autry was satisfied with my deli clerk position but questioned my arrangements.

"You drove here yourself?"

"Yeah," I said. "Bought a used Dodge. Making payments, I mean."

"How'd you get the apartment?"

"A friend of mine owns the building. He's letting me live there on the cheap."

Autry crossed his thick arms across his chest. He had a body like a retired football player and a nose that had been broken a time or two. His southern drawl was only noticeable when he used certain words, but when it surfaced it was rich and nauseating.

"This friend," he said. "Anyone I'd know?"

"He ain't a felon, if that's what you mean."

It was true enough. The owner was a criminal who'd never done hard time. One of Pino's cleaner associates.

"What's his name?" Autry asked, prodding just to throw his authority at me.

I gave him the name Pino had given me, an alias that could be backed up if the bull checked. Autry gave me the usual lecture about keeping on straight time, reminding me of all the times my old man had sat me down and orated about my bad behavior. I listened now about as much as I had back then.

"I've paid for my mistake," I told him. "I don't plan to repeat it. I'm thirty-three years old and starting a new life, fresh and clean."

"A significant age," Autry said, leaning on his desk. "Some call it the 'Jesus Year,' on account of him dyin' and being resurrected at age thirty-three. It's a year to focus on your growth as a person. Stop coastin' and start pedalin'."

I didn't know what the fuck he was talking about.

"Exactly," I said.

I knew Max Marino from before I'd gone to prison, a small-time hood who mostly dealt grass and played drugstore cowboy for opioids. I could've asked Pino to have someone hunt him down, but I didn't want Pino knowing I'd be buying drugs. Older guineas are weird about that. They'll put a bullet in a man but won't touch a bong. So I frequented some of the bars and old hangouts until I bumped into a mutual acquaintance who gave me Max's number, for a price, of course.

Max was surprised to hear from me. We hadn't been close friends—after my years overseas in the military, I was too fucked in the head for real relationships—but he'd been my dealer, helping me self-medicate my PTSD.

He agreed to meet me at a cramped joint called Olle's Pizza. We carried our slices to one of two tables outside, sitting across from the UPS store. The sunlight made Max squint. I noticed track marks on his arms.

"I deal heavier stuff now," he told me. "But I can still get you weed."

"Actually, I prefer coke these days."

"No sweat. Coke, uppers. Acid, mushrooms. I've got a stash in my car." When he pronounced *car* his Pride of Boston accent shined. "Wasn't sure what you'd be needing. Better not to take the weed I've got on hand. It's dirt. But the coke's wicked strong. I get it from this Irish mick up in Worcester there. Definitely better than any you woulda done in prison."

"So, you did time?"

"Shit yeah," he said. "A year for grass with intent to sell. A fuckin' *year* for *pot* in the *twenty first century*. I mean . . . what the fuck, right? But hey, whadda ya gonna do? Like old blue eyes says, *that's life*."

"We're both out now, man."

"And that's what's important, Jack. Freedom. To do whatever the fuck we want."

I laid out my new suit for my date with Natalie and ironed the shirt I'd bought. I was forgoing a tie, as I had never liked them. They always made me feel as if a small child was choking me. I polished my dress shoes—the same rich brown as the suit—and put my coiled leather belt on top of the dresser. My taste in clothes had matured since I'd been in prison. These were nice-looking but affordable.

I showered and shaved and groomed myself with Pinaud, the sort of simple pleasures Pino had spoke about. I trimmed my eyebrows with barber scissors but there was nothing I could do about the small scar that ran through one of them from where I'd been hit with a bottle in a bar fight a decade earlier. Another inch and I'd have lost the eye. My other scars were on my torso. Natalie wouldn't see those until we were farther along.

I took her to dinner at Mama Luna's, the same Italian restaurant Pino took me to on my first night out. I recommended the exact same course to her that he had to me. Natalie wore a simple green dress. A minor disappointment, but she was still attractive. Even more so than she was at work. A small crucifix hung on a thin, gold chain around her neck. She'd applied eyeshadow—something women didn't do as much as they should anymore—and I detected a hint of blush. Her eyes gleamed in the light of the candles. Even while admiring her beauty, I ascertained I was more handsome than she was beautiful, which meant I was probably better looking than most of the people she'd dated. That wasn't vanity talking. It was just the reality of sexual politics.

"I'm so glad you finally asked me out," she admitted.

"*Finally*? You'd been waiting?"

"Just a little while."

She was being playful, a side of her I hadn't glimpsed before. I advised the waiter to keep the wine coming. I learned she'd been engaged for two years but had never married or had children. She and her fiancé had decided to break up mutually, which I knew meant she'd had her heart broken, adding another weapon to my arsenal. I wondered if she was deliberately feeding me this information as a passive invite, but doubted she was clever enough for such mental swordplay. She had a degree in sociology that had done fuck all for her, and her parents lived in Avon. Her sister had a husband and three kids. When Natalie told me this little fact, there was a glint of sibling envy behind her eyes.

"Anyway, enough about me," she said. "Tell me about you."

"What do you wanna know?"

"Anything, really."

"Well, I've never been married either. Don't have any kids." This was true, but what I said next was a tactical lie. "I'd like to someday, if I find the right person."

She smiled, then looked away, bashful. The hot young hostess walked past but I forced myself to keep my attention on my date.

I took her to see the movie she'd picked. Some saccharine drivel about female friendship that left me zoning out. Natalie let me put my arm around her but I knew putting my hand on her leg would be too much too soon for this sort of girl. I would be lucky to get so much as a kiss tonight even though I was now certain Natalie wanted me to fuck her. That was all right with me. The ones who take things slow are more satisfying to break.

At the end of our date I walked her up to her apartment. A cat meowed from behind the door. When I leaned in to kiss her, she tried to give me her cheek but I turned her chin and kissed her on the lips—a small taste of the domination to come. My other hand on her arm, I felt that tender skin go gooseflesh. We said goodnight and I was heading down the stairs before she'd closed her door.

An hour later I was high on coke with a chubby Latino escort stripped and bent over my kitchen counter. Natalie had left my mind.

"I've got something for you," Pino said.

It was about time. I'd been slicing prosciutto for close to a month now, bringing home a measly five hundred a week. Any longer and I would have done something on my own.

I nodded. "That's great news."

"It's a truck job."

"Armored?"

He snorted a laugh. "What're you, nuts? No, nothing that intense. It's a simple truck job, Jackie, a delivery of electronics—4K TVs, that sort of thing."

"So I'll be driving hot items."

"You'll be *making* them hot. The deliveries come from a warehouse to one of those huge members-only retailers. You and another one of our guys will go to the warehouse tomorrow night. One of the receivers is our insider, but the other ain't in on it. He may or may not be there. If so, he'll need to be dealt with. But don't make it anything permanent. You'll have to rough up our inside guy too for appearances sake, but don't hurt him too bad. It just needs to look like they were attacked, that way no one thinks to tie either of them to the crime. You drive the truck. It's no more complicated than a U-Haul. My other guy takes off in the car you came in."

Our fat waitress checked on us and I ordered another beer. It was a clear, sunny afternoon and Pino and I sat at a sidewalk café. Bees congregated in a nearby flower garden and squirrels did the tightrope on power lines. A ring of sweat had formed around the collar of Pino's guayabera shirt. The lunch rush had passed and there were few patrons, so we could talk freely as long as we did so in hushed tones.

"Where's the drop off?" I asked.

He dabbed at his forehead with a napkin. "Waltham, Mass. We've got an industrial building we use for redistribution. There'll be a return car waiting for you there and an envelope on the seat. Leave the car at Giuseppe's. Keep the envelope. Simple."

For our fourth date Natalie invited me to her apartment. She was going to make me dinner. Both brought implications. For one thing she was letting me into her home, which hinted at sex, and for another thing she was cooking for me—a domestic act of affection underlined by a housewife-like level of subservience.

Her abode was small. The kitchen was just off the living room, a round table for two in between. There was only one bedroom, and the bathroom was attached so you had to walk through to get to it. Her cat was elderly and merely snoozed on the couch beside me as I watched Natalie work in her little apron. She wore jeans and a t-shirt, barefoot with her toenails freshly painted. She reminded me of Ginger with her hair pulled back in a ponytail. The last time I'd seen the tranny she was begging me not to give her to Mickey Blake because he had a reputation for being abusive, beating the girls for sexual kicks and pissing in their mouths.

"You'll drink every last drop," I told her.

"Please, Daddy," Ginger whined. "Don't leave me."

"You expect me to stay here now that I'm getting out tomorrow?"

"Daddy, please—"

I backhanded her, knocking free a goblet of snot. "You're my bitch. You'll work for who I tell you to work for whether I'm here or not, understand?"

Ginger began to sob. "Don't you love me anymore?"

I laughed from deep in my belly. Ginger's delusions were magnified by the reality of my release. That night I told her to blow me, and she did so sensually, as if savoring our last night together. After I came, I told her to keep my dick in her mouth and then pissed to prove a point. When she tried to pull away, I rabbit-punched her, forcing my dick and its stream down her throat. Afterward, she wretched over the shitter for a good twenty minutes but couldn't get anything up. Even after all that, she told me she would always love me. I told her to shut up so I could get some sleep.

"Smells good," I told Natalie.

She turned and smiled, spatula in hand. "White wine chicken and asparagus with little potatoes. I love the red ones."

"Me too," I said, though I didn't give a fuck.

I got off the sofa and joined her in the kitchen. She was sprinkling thyme when I came up behind her and slid my arms around her waist. This was the first time I'd embraced her like this. I blew in her ear and she giggled, her childlike nature making me hard. I slipped my hands beneath the apron, finding the sliver of exposed belly flesh between her shirt and her jeans, and ran one finger along it. She exhaled and I leaned into her neck, planting little kisses upon the nape. Natalie hummed my name. I slipped my hand under her shirt, but she motioned me away.

I froze, letting her speak first.

"Just . . . not right now," she said with a small smile. "I'm cooking." She kissed my cheek and went back to fucking with her spices.

I stepped back. On my way to the sofa I said, "Wear a dress next time."

My tone was matter of fact. Natalie turned only partly.

"Sorry?" she asked.

"You heard me." I picked up a magazine from the

coffee table. "You're wearing jeans. Next time, wear a dress."

She was still and silent. This was my first play at her and despite my evaluation her response could go a variety of ways. She'd been happy up to this point and made no attempts to hide it. I'd cured the loneliness left behind in the wake of her almost-husband's desertion. She was too terrified of that loneliness returning not to be malleable. So instead of any righteous, feminist indignation she just cast her eyes downward and gave a little nod.

"Sure," she said. "Okay."

It was all she said, and all I needed to hear.

That night I fucked her for the first time. She was tender but unskilled, even a little awkward. I had to guide her to do every little thing, despite keeping the sex conventional and not dipping into any of my usual perversions. I didn't even ask her for oral, for Christ's sake. She was also uncomfortable with words like "cock" and "pussy," substituting with toddler terms like "pee-pee" and "thingy." Not out of some sort of child fetish, but a genuine reluctance to talk dirty. She even wanted to keep her bra on—obviously because of her flat chest—another insecurity. I removed it despite her objections and deliberately paid no attention to what little tits she had, knowing my disinterest in them would cause Natalie further self-loathing in regards to her body.

Though she had the next day off, I had to open the deli in the morning and used this as an excuse to decline her invitation to stay the night. I told her I'd call her the next day but didn't. She called me late, naturally, asking if she'd done something wrong. I made up a story about having gone down for a nap after work and told her I wished I'd just stayed the night. I said I was sorry for not calling sooner but was just about to when my phone rang. I told her what a wonderful time I'd had, how I was glad our relationship had gone to this next level. I asked if she wanted to go to the fireworks festival the following night and her relief came in such a powerful surge I could almost feel it spill over and out through the phone. Just before we got off, I gave her a little reminder.

"Don't forget—wear a dress."

She didn't hesitate. "Absolutely, Jackie. I know just the one!"

I had her.

CHAPTER THREE

I WAS PAIRED up with a guy named Vin. He was tall but had a square, Nick Nolte face and a fat nose with busted capillaries. He could be forty or sixty. It took me a minute to realize he was the driver who'd picked me up from prison. He didn't talk much, which suited me fine. The less we knew about each other, the better. If either of us got pinched there'd be less for us to reveal to the cops.

All that code of honor horseshit you think gangsters have is more based in Hollywood than reality. At best it's a relic from a more dignified age. These days everyone's out for themselves in this world—and there's no coming back from that.

When we reached the warehouse, Vin had me pull the car around to the loading dock at the rear. Behind it was only a chain link fence and railroad tracks, perfectly deserted. Two delivery trucks were lined up to the receiving dock, facing backward to be loaded. A man in overalls smoked a cigarette on the concrete steps.

"That's our insider," Vin said.

He waved out the window and the dockworker approached our car, a slim weasel with a working class accent.

"Hey, guys. I'm Pau—"

I cut him off. "Don't tell us your fucking name."

He cleared his throat. "Okay. Listen. My coworker is here tonight after all."

Vin shook his head. "*Fangul.*"

"Not a problem," I said. "We were told it might come to this."

"Still a pain in my ass," Vin said.

The dockworker shrugged. "It is what it is. I know you gotta rough me up. Just not the face, okay?"

I got out of the car. "We need it to show, stupid. It has to be your face, 'less you want us to break a limb."

"Fuck that."

"Right then. Here's what we'll do—"

I gave him a quick, straight jab to the nose before he could see it coming. I followed with a left hook and the dockworker dropped to one knee, so I grabbed his hair and kneed him in the face. Blood misted from his nose. He hit the ground and I came up on him, ready to kick him in the face, but Vin took my arm and pulled me off.

"That's enough."

He was right. It was just hard to turn it off once it was on.

"Oh, Jesus," the dockworker mumbled.

"Better to get it over with quick," I told him.

"C'mon," Vin told the dockworker, holding out a hand. "Get up. We need you to show us around inside."

"But . . . it's all set to go."

"I said get up."

The dockworker wobbled to his feet. Vin brushed the grit from the man's back and patted his shoulders.

As we followed him up the steps, Vin drew a .22 pistol from his ankle holster, pointing it at the dockworker's back, feigning a hostage situation. Pino had gotten me a .38 snubnosed revolver but, despite their size, those guns are deafeningly loud, so Vin was the designated gunman tonight, whereas I was the muscle. Stepping into the doorway and behind a pallet of cardboard boxes wrapped in cellophane, the air conditioning chilled the sweat on the back of my neck, and I drew the pantyhose from my pocket and pulled them over my head. Vin did the same. We marched the dockworker to the loading bay where the receiver was writing on a clipboard, inventorying the boxes going onto the truck for shipment. When he looked up, he saw the dockworker first and started to say something about getting his ass in gear, then shut his mouth when we came into the light. He dropped the clipboard and put up both hands.

"Take what you want," he said. "Just don't hurt us."

I rushed him. He stepped back but I caught his shirt before he could flee down the hall and gave him a blow to the kidneys, spun him around, and clocked him one in the jaw.

He gasped. "Please . . . "

I hit him in the gut. He tried to squirrel away but didn't fight back. Disgusted, I slammed him into the wall, knocking mounted clipboards off their hooks and causing a bulletin board to fall and hit the guy on the top of his head. He reached up to cradle his skull and I took his arm and, in a snapping motion, tried to break it. He shrieked and started babbling about his family. I spun him onto the receiving desk and yanked that same arm all the way around his back. I heard something pop—possibly his elbow or shoulder—and he screamed like a little girl who'd just had a frog thrown down the back of her shirt.

"Enough already," Vin said, then whispered, "Nothing permanent, remember?"

I grabbed the gun they used to scan barcodes and broke it across the receiver's face, spattering blood and plastic and microchips. He slid to the floor, his bleary eyes filling with blood.

"Jesus," the other worker said. "Was that really necessary?"

I ignored him. I went to the truck and gave the freight the once over. The boxes bore all the names I was looking for—Sony, Bose, Samsung, Playstation. Tens of thousands worth of product. I closed the sliding door and secured the latch. Already the knuckles on my right hand were swelling. Should've worn gloves.

The dockworker stepped over the receiver and took the keys. He seemed a little too relaxed, so I elbowed him in the stomach so not to raise the receiver's suspicion about his coworker. He stumbled, just barely finding the chair.

Vin grumbled as we exited the building. I got into the truck and Vin took off in the car, tires screeching on the sharp turn around the side of the warehouse. The truck rumbled forward and in fifteen minutes I was on the highway. It was a hot night in July, and I drove with the windows down all the way to Waltham.

Pino held a barbeque for the fourth. The deli was closed so Natalie and I were able to go together. I told her to help Rosalie in the kitchen so Pino and I could chat alone while he grilled another round of shish kabobs and frankfurters.

"Thanks for putting me to work," I said.

"Don't go so fucking hard next time," he said, glowering. "Our inside guy lost a tooth. I made good. Told him I'd replace it, but I'll be taking it out of your next cut."

I nodded. "Fair enough."

"I already know you're tough as roofing nails, Jackie. I was in the joint with you, remember? You've got nothing to prove."

"Just got a little carried away is all."

"You got *a lot* carried away. Your parole officer sees that busted hand of yours and he'll be more than a little curious. Low profile!"

"You're right, Pino. Sorry."

He stared at me, then patted my shoulder. "Irregardless, you and Vin did good. Everybody was pleased with the haul. There'll be more work for you soon."

"Thanks, Pino—for everything. I owe you."

"Good to know." He grinned. "So, you and the deli girl . . ."

"Natalie."

"Yeah, Natalie. That's nice, real nice. Having a woman is good all around—for appearances especially, seeing as you were runnin' fags in the joint. Best to distance yourself from all that."

"Definitely."

"Speaking of, I got my first monthly from Mickey and it was a good number. You were right about him."

AND THE DEVIL CRIED

Rosalie came outside with a tray of watermelon slices. Natalie walked behind her, carrying a bag of buns. She favored one-piece bathing suits, but I'd bought her a bikini. She wanted to wear a little skirt with it, but I refused. Her ass was her best quality, and it was important to flaunt my property. She brought Pino the hot dog buns. I patted her on the rear just hard enough to make a smacking sound and told her to fetch me another Heineken.

Natalie giggled it off to hide her embarrassment. "Sure, Jackie."

She headed to the ice barrel where they were kept. One butt cheek had gone pink.

Pino nodded at me in approval. "You're doing it right, kid."

For Natalie's thirty-fifth birthday I had three dozen roses delivered to her apartment, took her to Mama Luna's for dinner, and gave her an elegant bracelet. (Five hundred retail, but I got it for half through Pino's jewelry guy.) I thought she might cry right there in the restaurant. I stayed the night, and in the morning made sure to scold her for burning the bacon and serving runny eggs—both of which were actually fine—and then left in a huff, slamming the door behind me. She apologized profusely that night, and I had her suck my dick for the first time. I allowed her to spit in the sink this time. Going forward, I would make her swallow.

I began hinting about her getting breast implants. Though she didn't show enthusiasm, she didn't argue either. I considered tattoos and piercings as well—more body modifications under my control—but decided against them because I hated the look of all that bar whore trash. Besides, surgery was much more demanding. I would actually be putting her *under the fucking knife*.

I started doing collections for Pino and he had Giuseppe trim my hours at the deli. Pino paid me from the vigs made on the loans and I only got rough with the payees when they too frequently came up short. Easy work. It didn't take up much of my time and was relatively low risk. So not to cause suspicion from Hugh Autry, I stayed in the same modest apartment, but furnished it with my new income. I bought new clothes, both for Natalie and myself. She came with me to the shops, but I picked out the dresses and shoes I wanted for her, as well as lingerie. She could wear her jeans and t-shirts at work. Otherwise, her appearance had to meet my standards at all times—even in her own home. We ended up numbering the outfits so I could simply text her which one I wanted her in.

"It's bad," Vin told me. "Real bad."

"What the hell happened?"

"Not over the phone. Come down to the bar."

The Chimney was a small, dark bar made to resemble an English pub. I arrived twenty minutes later to find Vin sitting on a stool, sipping scotch with a haggard expression. Just looking at him made my stomach go hollow. I sat beside him and ordered a belt of bourbon. Just before noon—a little early for me, but I suspected I was going to need it.

"So what is it?" I asked.

"It's bad, Jackie."

"Yeah, you said. What is it, feds?"

He shook his head and took another sip. Was he trying to be cinematic here or was it just that difficult to talk about? Either way I was growing impatient. I never liked to be kept waiting. Vin and I had gotten to know each other now that we'd pulled off a few jobs together. I didn't consider him a friend exactly, but we had a moderate rapport. There was no reason for him to be clandestine.

"Pino have a heart attack or something?" I asked.

Vin shook his head again. "Nah. He's fine physically and there's no cops involved. It's worse than that, Jackie. It's about his kid."

I thought of Drea. The last time I'd seen her was at the barbeque. She'd been wearing cut off jean shorts and a pink bikini top—fucking *pink*, the color that makes me foam.

"What's wrong with her?" I asked.

"Not the girl. Pino's son—Bobby."

Of course. The portly pre-teen who liked pool noodle fights.

"Okay," I said. "What happened? Spit it out already, would ya? I've gotta go to work on Tuesday."

Vin sighed. "Bobby was hit by a car while riding his bike. The driver was shitfaced drunk. Slammed into the kid, throwing him under the wheels."

"Ah, shit. Is the kid hurt bad?"

Vin's eyes were flint. "Bobby's dead, Jackie."

I put my glass down on the bar and stared into it.

I didn't exactly feel for Pino or his fat-ass kid. This did, however, raise concerns about my cash flow. If Pino were grieving with his family would my jobs go dry? How long would he be out? I supposed I would still have the collections, but it made me anxious anyway.

"How's Pino taking it?" I asked.

"How the fuck do you think? He's beside himself. A total train-wreck. I've known the man twenty-six years and this is the first time I've ever seen him cry."

I bit my lip and shook my head at the floor—my best attempt at an empathetic expression. "Such a tragedy. When are the services?"

"Saturday," Vin said. "They're hoping an open casket can happen, but from what I've been told the poor kid was shredded. Dragged across the asphalt, face pulped."

"Jesus. Poor Pino . . . oh man, poor Rosalie."

"She wouldn't even come out of the bedroom when I came by. I could hear her screaming from the front lawn."

My brow furrowed. "She was actually screaming?"

Vin nodded. "About the driver. She wants the son of a bitch killed."

The sunshine seemed inappropriate for such a serious meeting. There was not a single cloud as Pino, Vin, and I sat at the poolside table. Pino was gray and wan. Purple bags cradled his eyes and he appeared to have lost weight, his grief eating him like cancer. It'd been only a couple weeks since he'd put his son in the ground, but he seemed to have aged ten years. Cigar smoke poured from his nostrils.

"He made bail," Pino said.

"Already?" Vin asked.

I leaned in. "It's a fuckin' disgrace, Pino."

"I go to prison for racketeering," Pino said, "but they release a child-killer just like that. Cocksucker has two prior DUI arrests. Ya believe this?"

Vin and I said nothing, just waited.

"His name's Davidson," Pino told us. "From Hartford. Forty years old and lives with his mother, the fuckin' loser."

Silence fell between us. The leaves rustled against the sky like pompoms. The pool filter hummed. Rosalie had voluntarily checked into a wellness center and Drea was at her grandmother's. Pino's emptiness was palpable, almost thick enough to grab in your fist.

"I'll do it," I said.

Pino flicked his cigar and the ash vanished into the breeze. "Nah, Jackie. Not him."

I looked to Vin, but he was equally confused.

"Davidson," Pino said, "has a daughter."

CHAPTER FOUR

NATALIE HID HER face into my chest as the teenager was ripped in half. She always said she didn't like horror movies, but I knew she enjoyed them because it gave her an opportunity to snuggle into me like I was her big protector, some knight from the fairy stories of her childhood. She had a lot of fantasies and delusions. That's one of the reasons she wanted to introduce me to her parents, who'd invited us to dinner at their house that coming weekend.

I zoned out as the CGI frights continued on the big screen, thinking about my meeting with Vin by the overpass. He'd called and asked me to come out there, and when I arrived we sat in his car for a chat. He kept it running for the air conditioning. The day's humidity was excruciating.

"You can't do this, Jackie," he said.

"No offense, Vin, but you don't pay my bills."

He popped a cigarette in his mouth and offered me one. We lit up and Vin cracked the windows.

"I looked into it," he said. "Eleven, Jackie."

"Pino's boy was just a year older."

"Pino's boy was an accident."

"Tell Rosalie that."

He exhaled. "Wait it out. Pino will come to his

senses. His head's all messed up right now is all. He's bereaved and emotional, raging without thinking. Once he cools off, he won't want this."

"All the more reason for me to do it now, before the money's off the table."

Vin's eyes went cold. "You're a selfish son of a bitch, aren't you?"

"Business is business."

"It might be the last payday you ever see."

I held his stare. "You threatening me, Vin?"

"No, you idiot. I'm trying to tell you if you do this you may find yourself blacklisted or worse. If the higher-ups find out Pino ordered this hit, he'll be out. Finished. Then where will you be?"

"They're not going to find out. The only person who might tell them is you, and if you snitch I'll kill you next."

His eyes went cold again. "Don't you threaten me either, Jackie. I'm no rat. I'm trying to help you here. More than that I'm trying to help that little girl. I'd gladly choke that drunk with my own two hands for running over Bobby, but I cannot abide his daughter being murdered because of his recklessness. It ain't right."

I shrugged, blowing smoke. "Who's to say what's right, Vin?"

A waft of heat came through the cracked window, moistening my brow. I gazed at the muddy stream under the bridge, squinting against the glare coming off the Lincoln's hood. On the concrete pillar closest to us someone had spray-painted a huge cock and balls and scrawled *SUCK IT*. I stirred. Vin's bad side was someplace I didn't want to be. Not that I was afraid of him, I just preferred to keep my business dealings diplomatic.

"Look, Vin, this thing is complex," I told him. "Pino doesn't want it to be an obvious hit. The cops will come right to his door if this girl gets run over or shot in the head. I've got to find a way that'll look clean and raise as few eyebrows as possible. This'll take time. Hopefully by then Pino will call it off. If not, you know I have no choice but to follow the boss' orders. Just know I won't take any pleasure in it, okay?"

But I wasn't sure that was true. Like anything else, whether or not it would be pleasurable would depend on how it all unfurled.

When the movie ended, Natalie and I went to my place. I was accruing more possessions and was hardly ever at the deli anymore. I told her I'd taken a job selling health insurance. She was very proud of me.

At this point I'd stopped initiating sex with her. When she tried to initiate it, I only gave in half the time, making her earn it by doing increasingly dirtier things. I wasn't growing tired of her—in fact, because of the manipulations, I was now more excited than ever to take her to bed—but I needed her to believe she bored me. That night she stayed over. I allowed her to seduce me and went at her with enthusiasm to build up her hopes. After a few minutes, I withdrew from her with a sigh.

"I'm sorry," I said. "I'm just not feeling it tonight."

This wasn't the first time I'd faked failure. Natalie sat up. Even in the darkness I could detect the panic on her face, the moonlight making her teary eyes shine.

"Just tell me what you want, baby," she said. "Whatever you want."

I exhaled. "You'd never do it. Just go to sleep."

Natalie was still and silent, then she straddled me in sexual desperation, grinding into me and kissing my nipples. Staying flaccid was difficult, so I scooted back from the friction.

"Anything you want, baby," Natalie said, nearly a whimper. "I just want you to be happy with me."

I sat up and stroked strands of hair from her face, patting her like the pet she had become.

"Are you sure?" I asked.

"Of course, baby. I love you."

Words she said frequently but I usually avoided, keeping them few and far between to keep my little Natalie forever uncertain. It was important to her to love me, because she needed that in her life. She'd convinced herself of it. Now that she was taking me to see her parents, there was even more pressure on her to maintain the relationship. She didn't want to face her parents with yet another failure.

I kissed her passionately, biting her lip just so. She shivered.

"Roll onto your stomach," I told her.

She did so gingerly. I put a pillow under her hips, arching her ass in the air, and opened the nightstand for the massage oil she used to rub my back.

A man experiences several pleasures when sodomizing a woman. It's tighter and surprisingly warmer than vaginal sex. But the true allure is that it is more degrading—at least for women like Natalie. She was so conventional in bed, the sexual equivalent to skim milk. Her awkwardness was preceded by prudishness, some deep-set value system I had to chip away at, using her own feelings of inadequacy to make her feel obligated to go to places she didn't want to.

Obviously, she was an anal virgin. As I dabbed her rectum with oil, I told her I'd be gentle.

I was at first.

Then I wasn't.

Woodrow Elementary School wouldn't reopen until the end of August. I had to find another way to stalk Seri Davidson. She lived with her mother—Roy's ex-wife Carmen—and had no siblings. From what I could tell, there was no stepdad or boyfriend or anyone else living at their modest house in Plainville. A garden gnome by the front steps stood guard over a flowerbed lined with miniature American flags, leftovers from the fourth. Three houses down on the other side of the street stood an empty colonial with a *for rent* sign on the lawn. I parked there and watched Seri's house, waiting for any sign of the child. She was in those awkward tween years when they don't play outside much, but I hoped to catch her coming and going.

I ended up seeing her mother first.

Carmen was an anthropomorphic bear—a saggy, overweight woman with short hair and Play-Doh limbs. She had a pretty face, making her obesity all the more a shame. As she walked out to her car, I noticed a waitress apron tied around her generous waist. At least two of me would have fit in those jeans.

AND THE DEVIL CRIED

I followed her to an Applebee's. Her enormous ass cheeks heaved in revolting undulations as she walked inside. I waited fifteen minutes until I was sure she was working, then drove back to her house. For just such an opportunity, I'd worn one of my suits and had swiped a stack of religious pamphlets from a local church.

The gnome glared at me as I rang the doorbell, his candy eyes chipped and faded by too many seasons out here all alone. Beside him, an anthill swarmed with war. I watched the windows for any change in light and shadow, any sign of life. There was no car in the driveway and there'd been nothing to indicate a babysitter. Eleven was old enough to be home alone, wasn't it? I supposed it depended on the maturity level of the child. Girls tend to mature faster than boys but they're also more likely to be victims of violent crimes. Seri's father was a deadbeat drunk, but that didn't mean her mother was equally neglectful. Still, childcare gets expensive, and you've got to cut the cord sometime.

The weight of my sport coat was stifling under the midday sun. I fanned myself with the Jesus pamphlets and leaned toward the window. No lights or televisions or music. Nothing but brown shadows. If someone was home, they were conserving more electricity than your average American. Clearing my throat, I spat a globule into the frenzy of the ants, their black bodies scrambling about the pyramid. I walked around the side of the house where the grass was brown and unattended. An air conditioning unit hung out one window, but despite the blazing day it wasn't running. I looked back and forth, cautious of any nosy neighbors, then slowly, cautiously, pushed the AC unit upward just to see if it would budge. It rose off the windowsill and I gently guided it back down into place.

I returned to my car and drove off.

Now I had a way inside.

I spent the afternoon researching rat poisons on Natalie's computer. They were an option, but their efficacy varied when it came to human toxicity. Seri would have to ingest large amounts over long periods of time and a long illness would come first. I didn't care if the little girl suffered, but I did want this done quickly, before Pino had second thoughts. But the only way to successfully poison someone with over-the-counter pesticide was by rationing it out. Such murders tended to be committed by the caregivers of the victim. So poisoning was out, unless I could score some hard thallium or strychnine. But it wasn't as if I knew any retired KGB agents or snake-handling ministers.

A simple break-in would work, I thought. The family of Dennis Kingsley—the first man I'd ever killed—had never seen justice served or gotten any closure. He was just an old man who'd been randomly killed in a burglary. Sad, but it happens. Carmen and her daughter could meet a similar fate, but I didn't want to kill Carmen if I didn't have to. If you're good at something, never do it for free. Besides, one target is much simpler than two. The fewer people you have to hit in an assassination, the better. I'd learned that in the army, blowing the scalps off sand niggers with sniper rifles. I wondered if Pino could get his hands on a Barrett. Then I could pluck the little girl from a thousand yards away, separating her pigtails with a devastating .50 BMG round. I was envisioning the child's detonating skull when Natalie came up behind me and draped her arms over my shoulders.

"What're you doing, honey?" she asked, looking at the screen.

I closed the browser window and patted her arm. "Nothing."

"Mice in your apartment?"

"Not in mine, but in the building. The landlord is taking care of it, but I was curious about any chemical side effects."

"That's 'cause you're my big, healthy guy," she said, giving my bicep a squeeze.

Having now seen pictures of her ex-fiancé, I knew I was not only more handsome than him, but also better built. Though I didn't care about health food, Natalie assumed I was into nutrition because of my muscular frame and my insistence she stick to the diet I'd planned out for her. For days now she'd been eating according to my rules. I kept hoping to catch her with a hidden candy bar wrapper or something just so I could stress my disappointment, but either she was being extremely careful or extremely obedient. Given the work I'd put into her so far, neither would come as a surprise.

Not that Natalie needed to diet. She was a healthy weight and looked tasty in that bikini. I had other motives. Many cult leaders provide their followers only bland, low-protein foods while the leader enjoys lavish feasts. It's just another way to separate *you* from *them*.

"Did you tell your mother your diet restrictions?" I asked. "We don't want her making something you can't have tomorrow night."

Natalie stood up straight and bit her bottom lip. Bashful girl about to ask a favor.

"No exceptions," I told her.

"But baby," she said, "I've been so good. Can't we just make it a cheat day?"

I rose from the desk and placed my hands on her upper arms. I gave her the stare that always made her drop her eyes. They were hooded today in blue eyeshadow, the kind she knew I liked.

"Cheating on a diet is stealing from yourself," I said. "If a young man cheats on all his college exams he'll get a diploma, but he'll still be a dunce." A glib analogy but I knew she wouldn't question it. I threw her something more bumper sticker friendly. "No pain, no gain."

"I know," she said with a childlike pout. "It's just that Mom makes this incredible lasagna she likes to serve to guests. I told her how you'd like that, being Italian and all."

"I'm sure it's delicious." I shrugged, giving her a farm boy grin. "Tell you what, baby. She can make lasagna as long as you think you'll be strong enough to just stick to the salad. I don't want to tempt you when you're doing so well."

She beamed, as if she'd won something. "No, no, I'll be fine. You're so sweet to consider my feelings. Mom will be so happy if you like it, and I just know you will. Thanks, Jackie."

AND THE DEVIL CRIED

She stood on her toes and gave me a kiss on the cheek, bouncing with the excitement of bringing her new man home to the folks. In her simple mind a Hallmark movie was filming. Natalie was daring to dream—a gamble with low odds, a sucker bet if there ever was one. Once again she was stepping up to the great craps table of love only to play the field.

We snuggled up on the couch and watched half of a movie. Some Adam Sandler comedy my girlfriend found amusing. I laughed when it seemed appropriate and thought about Seri Davidson and her hippo mother and their shitty little house. Natalie paused the movie to prepare dinner. She made me steak and those little red potatoes of hers. For herself, she made a salad without cheese or dressing.

When she put the plates in front of us, I took her by the wrist before she could sit down.

"Get under the table," I said.

She blinked. "What, baby?"

I scooched my chair back. "Get down on all fours."

I recognized the worry that flashed across her face, that pale look of horror and disgust she got whenever I wanted anal sex.

"Facing me," I assured her.

"Jackie," she said. "What're you—"

"Do it," I said, pulling her down.

I positioned her under the table with her head in my lap, just below my plate. I cut into my steak—bloody rare, perfect. My girlfriend, still inhibited despite all I'd taught her, just stayed there on the floor like a dog awaiting table scraps. I undid my belt and initiated everything, guiding her once again. She fellated me as I ate my dinner, drops of meat juice falling into her hair with my every bite. I turned the stupid movie back on, and this time my laughter was genuine.

I followed Carmen and Seri when they left the house together. I only briefly got a glimpse of the girl as she'd skipped—actually fucking *skipped*—along to the car. Limp brunette hair. Gangly arms and long legs, completely out of proportion with the rest of her. Denim overalls, the shorts ending in rollups, baggy as a camping tent on her prepubescent form. She was a scrawny girl. Must have gotten that from her old man, lucking out by only inheriting her mother's face.

They pulled into a Wal-Mart and I parked in front of the nearby hair salon, waiting for them to enter the store before getting out of my car. I caught up with them in women's clothing, hiding just behind a wall of bagged socks. It seemed they were doing some back to school shopping. A girl that age must outgrow her clothes every year. Even now they kept going back and forth between the women's and girl's sections. Browsing t-shirts, Carmen got a call and wandered off with her phone in one ear and her finger in the other, leaving Seri to shop on her own.

I moved through racks of jeans like a rattlesnake through tall grass, stalking my oblivious prey. I looked to the dressing rooms. The attendant was gone. I scanned the department. Only a granny in a motor scooter all the way down by the shoes, trying to jam a fluffy slipper over a foot wrapped in a diabetic sock. Carmen had disappeared, probably in search of a better signal. Seri continued to sift through the shirts as I stepped up to the rack on the other side. I slid one hanger across after another, not even looking at the clothes they carried, my eyes locked on the girl. She still hadn't looked up at me. Retail establishments give a groundless illusion of safety.

When at last she noticed me, Seri looked away the very second our eyes met, not even giving me a polite smile. But I'd seen her face up close now. The puffy lower lip. The overstated eyelashes. The baby fat that still clung to her cheeks. The face of a cherub on the body of a corn maze scarecrow.

Seri moved to the table of folded sweaters, running her fingertips along the material as she passed them by. I maneuvered through the displays so not to alarm her, creating distance only to forge a natural path. I paused at a stand of clear buckets filled with brightly colored panties decorated with cute images of unicorns, cupcakes, bumblebees, and a wide variety of hearts.

It's always Valentine's Day under a little girl's skirt.

Seri reached for one of the sweaters and held it up. *Pink.*

My chest went tight, hairs rising across my body. The cool touch of the store's air conditioning now seemed arctic. Seri put the sweater close to her body, draping it over her torso like she was tucking herself into bed. All the moisture left my mouth.

That's when she looked up at me. Our eyes met and this time she smiled. I balled my fists to keep from screaming and forced myself to smile back, nod, and look away. Like a bumbling fool in some British comedy, I turned to the panty buckets as if I were shopping them. My hands seemed to move through them without my permission. My knuckles were the color of bone, but my palms had grown clammy.

I watched the girl from the corner of my eye. She now held a purple sweater up to her flat chest, the pink one slung over her shoulder. A malevolent heat rose through my guts.

The pink one, I urged her silently. *Pick the pink one.*

When I dared to look up again, she had a sweater in each hand, weighing them like a miniature Lady Justice. I hissed, shooting my thoughts at her like flaming arrows.

You stupid bitch. The pink one! Choose the pink one. Fucking bitch!

She put the pink sweater over her shoulder and began folding the purple one. The tear that ran down my cheek made me realize I hadn't been blinking.

Seri's mother came down the aisle. "Find something you like, hon?"

Seri held up the pink sweater with eyes aglow.

I walked out of the clothing department in search of the restrooms. Both stalls were occupied in the men's room, so I threw up in the urinal.

CHAPTER FIVE

"**So, Natalie tells** me you're a military man."

Paul Moore and his wife sat across from my girlfriend and I, a barrier of wine glasses between us. As promised, Lillian had made her famous lasagna, which I was enjoying despite having to listen to her incessantly talk about it. She was more assertive than her daughter, the kind of bitch whose nose is always slightly turned up as if savoring the smell of her own cunt. It was easy to steer her into talking about herself. Natalie's father, on the other hand, wanted to know more about me.

"That's right," I said. "I was in the army for eight years."

"Stationed?"

"Iraq first. Then Qatar."

"Where's that exactly?"

"Off the Persian Gulf."

"So, Afghanistan then?" Lillian asked.

I smiled. "Close enough."

Beside me, Natalie was as tight as a guitar string. I wasn't sure who embarrassed her more. Knowing her, it could be any of us—including herself. She smiled, teeth streaked with lipstick. She was still getting used to wearing it regularly.

"See any action?" Paul asked.

Natalie gasped. "Daddy!"

"Paul," Lillian said, "what a thing to ask a guest."

He shrugged at me. "You don't mind do ya?"

"Of course he minds, dad!"

I touched my girlfriend's arm. "It's okay, Nat."

My attention returned to Paul. Was he testing me or just that obtuse?

"Yeah," I said. "I saw my share of action."

In my memory, a hail of sniper fire peppered brown men as they fled from smoldering caves. They collapsed into the sand, screaming as wet flesh popped off their torsos.

Paul nodded, waiting. I knew what he wanted me to ask him, but I didn't.

"I was in the navy," he said.

A woman shrieking beneath me as I ripped away her abaya, her brother trying to keep his insides from exiting the wound I'd put in his stomach. While dying, he was forced to watch what I did to his sister.

"Four years," Paul said. "Of course, it wasn't wartime then . . . "

A hospital swallowed in blinding flame. Women sobbing as they tried to rescue babies mutated at birth by the depleted uranium in our ammunition.

" . . . still, the navy is a tough branch . . . "

A mortar round going off nearby, the vibrations mirroring a punch in the solar plexus.

"Oh, Paul," Lillian interrupted. "Would you stop with the navy already?"

He frowned. "Can't a man be proud of his service to his country?"

"Darling, we're all proud of you. We just don't want to talk about war while we're eating."

I imagined Paul in his Navy days, wearing his faggoty white cap as he pranced around NSB New London, getting shitfaced at strip clubs on the weekends, a hundred and seventy pounds of American pride.

"All right, fine," he said. "But you two ladies just don't understand. There's a bond between servicemen. It's like a big brotherhood. We vets take pride in all we've done."

"Hear, hear!" I said, raising my glass in toast.

Under the table, Natalie patted my leg in a silent apology. Her father's behavior clearly mortified her and I'm sure in some way she'd braced herself for this. She would expect to owe me something special tonight, and I would take full advantage.

"Only battle these two will ever fight," Paul said, pointing at the women, "is the battle of the bulge."

He pointed at his belly and winked at me. I'd always hated when guys winked when they were kidding. Lillian lightly batted her husband's arm, but behind her eyes boiled the sort of indignation only decades wasted on an unsatisfying marriage can brew. Natalie clanked her fork down on her salad plate and abruptly excused herself to the bathroom.

"Nat, c'mon," Paul said, but his daughter left the table.

"Why must you upset her every time she visits?" Lillian asked.

"She's too sensitive, Lily. We know this. I'm sure you've noticed this already too, huh, Jack?"

Lillian answered for me. "He's noticed no such thing."

She leaned over the table, scooped another square of lasagna, and plopped it upon my plate. I stabbed it with my fork.

"Good, huh?" Lillian said, only it wasn't a question. "I use three different kinds of meat."

I smiled as I chewed.

The night was going swimmingly.

I could have killed Seri Davidson that day in the Wal-Mart. I'd had the opportunity, but not the means. It wasn't like I was packing a hypodermic full of bleach or anything. I wasn't even sure what I intended to do when I followed her and her mother there. I would have loved to drag her to the dressing room and strangle her with the sleeves of that fucking sweater. Instead, I'd only watched in an inexplicable fever—a strange combination of nausea and pure captivation, bile at the back of my throat while at the same time my testicles drew closer to my body. I'd left the store immediately and gone home and taken a long, hot shower, sitting in the tub with my head hung between my legs. I slammed back a few shots of bourbon and went down for a nap before picking up Natalie for our dinner date with dear old Mom and Dad. But I couldn't sleep at all. I only lay there swimming in a black pit of daydreams.

"Thank you for tonight," Natalie said as I drove us home. She'd calmed down since her crying jag in the bathroom. We'd even stayed for cheesecake. "I know they can be a lot."

"I had a great time with Paul and Lillian," I said, which was a true.

AND THE DEVIL CRIED

"Sorry about my dad and the whole military thing. He thinks he's G.I. Joe. I just didn't think he would be so intrusive."

It was a trait Natalie didn't share with the old man. I'd told her of my military service mostly as a means to explain all my scars, but it's also a nice card to have in your deck when you're courting a young lady. Most Americans treat those who've served with automatic respect and women are attracted to men who are shown admiration by others. People in this country love a soldier . . . until he's at an intersection begging for booze money to wash the screams out of his head. Some men join the military out of a sense of honor or heritage. Others seek to build themselves into something better. Truth is, joining the service just comes down to simple stupidity. I'd signed on to the army at the age of eighteen—too immature to buy a wine cooler but just adult enough to get shot at in a foreign land, liberating nothing but oil.

I'd been trying to avoid jail. I had scared myself into believing it was only a matter of time before the police hunted me down for killing Dennis Kingsley. I was certain I would serve a life sentence, all for a lousy forty-two dollars. And so I'd foolishly sent myself into an institution that takes away even more of your personal freedom than a fucking prison. And, as if that wasn't a sturdy enough kick in the balls, they threw me—in all my aged wisdom—into a land on fire to fight religious maniacs who weren't afraid to die. Wagering my blood for every drop of fossil fuel, my country taught me there was little value to human life, but high value in murder. They paid me less than I would have made working retail and, once I was deemed too fucked up to continue butchering in their slaughterhouses, I was discharged and sent back to a homeland that was now more alien to me than my desert Hell. And when its citizens learned of my former vocation they said, "thank you for your service" and gave me ten percent off a burger two days a year.

I'd sacrificed myself. More fodder for the great, industrial war machine. Where's the honor in that? Guys like Paul Moore wear their little flag pins on their lapels. The rest of us have our stars in the form of exit wounds. Our stripes are our scars, the worst of which you can't even see.

The true face of the American serviceman is something you'll never find on a recruitment poster.

You're far more likely to see it in a mugshot.

CHAPTER SIX

"**HERE YOU GO**, hon," Carmen said, placing chicken tenders and fries upon the table.

I smiled. "I love it when a pretty woman calls me 'hon'."

She seemed briefly stunned, then gave me the customer service smile. "You want another Heineken?"

I nodded. "Thanks, darlin."

Carmen walked along the row of booths, her arm fat dimpling as she carried the tray. I had dressed in my most attractive suit—gray with a crisp, cream-colored shirt by Ralph Lauren—and had splashed on cologne. I'd added sexy George Michael stubble and a Cartier watch that could pay her rent for months. She returned to my booth with the beer, lingering a little, making small talk. The dinner rush had not yet begun.

"There should be a ring on that finger," I told her.

She blushed. "*You* are a big flirt."

"My name's Leo," I said, extending my hand.

She offered me her doughy paw. "Carmen. Nice to meet you, Leo."

"The pleasure's all mine." I slid my fingertips over her hers as we let go. "It's been a while since I've been to an Applebee's. I had no idea what I was missing."

She gave me a coy smile and a bat of the eyelashes. "Anything else I can get you?"

Your daughter.

"Yeah," I said. "Those digits."

She grinned, looking like a squirrel storing nuts in its cheeks. She glanced back and forth, as if to make sure the coast was clear, took her pen from behind her ear, and jotted down her number. She folded the paper and slid it across the table to me. I put my hand over hers.

"And so it began," I said.

A week into dating Carmen, Vin came to see me. I dreaded he would tell me the hit on Seri was off. Thankfully, this was not the case. I poured us bourbons with cola, which we took to the living room. Pale sunlight fell across us, illuminating the tiny dust particles in the air.

"Gil Yakel," he said. "He's a stubborn Jew who's very late on his loan payments. Keeps bemoaning the two-point vig, making excuses about having to spend all his money on his sick, old mother. Typical 'I just don't have it' horseshit."

"You wanna go say hello."

"And I need a second man. Yakel's nothing, but he's got two sons big as the Klitschko brothers."

"Who?"

"Ukrainian boxers."

"Funny thing about the big, athletic types. You hit 'em in the face with a baseball bat and they drop just like anybody else."

Vin snickered. It surprised me. He wasn't the sort of man who laughed. Something had hardened him years ago, something he was incapable of coming back from.

"The boys may or may not be there," he said. "One is about twenty or so and still lives at home. The other's on his own but lives in the same building. Anyhow, I'll compensate you for your time."

"All right. When you wanna go?"

After finishing our drinks, Vin drove us to a tenement building. Gil Yakel was the landlord and had an apartment on the third floor. It was a warm day but I wore a blazer to hide my shoulder holster. I also put on gloves so not to leave prints and protect my knuckles, having learned my lesson from the truck hijacking. I wished Vin had chosen more intimidating attire. In his kakis and polo shirt he looked more ready for a round of nine holes than an ass kicking. When we reached Gil's front door, though, Vin demonstrated his grit by kicking it in. Gil tried to slam it shut at the sight of us, but we pushed our way into the room with ease. Vin grabbed the Jew by his collar and slammed him into the wall. A small, decorative shelf fell, dangling from one hook, dropping porcelain knickknacks that exploded upon the hardwood floor.

Vin scowled. "I want my fucking money."

"I'm working on getting it for you," Gil said. "I just need a little more—"

Vin slugged him in the gut. Out of the corner of my eye I saw movement. A young, muscle-bound man charged into the anteroom, his fists like hams.

"Get the fuck off my dad!" he said.

I yanked the shelf from the wall and came at him

with it, swinging like a caveman. He tried to grab it and I faked right, then swung high, bashing him across the chin. He fell backward, tripping on the umbrella stand, and I swung again, breaking the shelf over the big Jew's back.

Vin hit Gil again. "See? That golem you call a son can't save you, understand?"

To emphasize this, I stomped on the son's balls. Squealing, he grabbed my ankle and dragged me to my knees and clipped me with a right hook to the face. I drew my .38 and pistol-whipped him across the nose. Blood burst from his face like paintball splatter. Though Herculean in appearance, the son was young and obviously had little to no experience fighting.

"Stewart!" Gil called out. "Please, Vin, leave my boy alone."

"The money, Gil," Vin said. "Twenty-four hours. Otherwise we take it out of your kid's ass. Make a reverse Yentl out of him."

"It's almost the first of the month. All the rent checks will come in. I'll pay, I'll pay."

"Four-point vig."

"Four?" Gil grimaced. "That's double what we—"

"Late fees. Now gimme what you got on hand."

Vin walked Gil through the apartment. I kept my pistol on Stewart. Not that it was needed. The kid was down hard. He'd need his nose to be reset, maybe a few stitches.

There was a sudden yell, followed by a gunshot. I came into the living room, both hands on my revolver. Someone screamed and I followed the sound to the open doorway of the master bedroom. A large man lumbered in the jam, an automatic pistol in his hand.

He was saying something about "the other one" when I came up behind him and shot him twice in the back. Ropes of blood spun toward me and when he hit the floor I planted a bullet through his skull, sending brain matter out his forehead. One eye dislodged and hung from the socket like a deflated birthday balloon. His father sobbed his name as I stepped over the carcass, cautious of the pooling gore. Gil was white as a blizzard. Vin was on the floor, leaning against the wall and clutching his stomach, blood seeping through his fingers. He sweated profusely, his face knotted in bright red pain. Above him, a wall safe hung open, a painting pushed aside.

"You," I said, pointing my gun in Gil's face. "Call 911. Tell them my friend here's been gut shot."

Gil was a blubbering mess. He fell to one knee, reaching for his dead-as-dog-shit son. I cracked the top of his skull with the butt of the revolver. He put out his hands to catch himself and slid through his eldest boy's blood and fell with a wet splat, his head just inches from what remained of his son's face. I moved quickly. There'd been too much noise already and now everyone was screaming. I stepped past Vin and removed the two stacks of wrapped bills from the safe. There was a golden bracelet, two pair of diamond earrings, a felt ring box, and some old stamps in a plastic sheet. I took them too.

Vin grabbed the leg of my jeans, hissing his words through clenched teeth. "Get me . . . outta . . . here."

"I'm calling for an ambulance."

"Can't go to . . . hospital . . . fuckin' cops."

"It's that or die, Vin, and die slow from the looks of it."

His eyes twitched with panic. "Just get me . . . to my car."

"Down three flights of stairs and across the street to where we parked? I don't think so."

I stepped away. Gil was sobbing with his head on his son's shoulder. I shot him in the head, the hollow point ending his patriarchal misery. I returned to Vin, pulled his phone from his pocket, and put it in his lap. I took his car keys, raised his trouser leg, and undid the gun holster, putting it and the .22 in the pocket of my blazer.

"Call 911," I said. "Tell them you were visiting your friend Gil when someone you'd never seen before came in to rob him and started shooting. Say it was a black guy. Cops always buy that. Tell them the spook started shooting and Yakel's boy here hit you by mistake in the crossfire. I'll take care of the other kid out there so no one can contradict your story."

"Jackie don't," he said. "Don't leave me here."

"You know I have to, Vin. You fucking know that."

"Please . . . I don't wanna die . . . not alone."

"And I don't wanna go back to prison."

I walked out of the bedroom, ignoring his pitiful cries. I'd done everything I could for the poor bastard. Holding his hand wouldn't save him, only doom me. Fuck that.

When I reached the anteroom, I froze at the bloody spot where I'd left Stewart. The goddamned kid was gone. The front door hung open. I holstered my .38, switching it out for Vin's quieter .22 revolver, and stormed out of the apartment in a steady stride, teeth grinding. Drops of blood were sprinkled upon the floor like a trail of breadcrumbs I followed to the elevator. The doors had already closed and the down arrow was lit up green.

A woman shrieked. She'd poked her damn fool head out of her apartment to see what all the commotion was about.

You know what they say about curious cats and the punishment they meet.

It pays to have military sniper training when you need to shoot someone from a distance. I fired only once. The bullet entered her eye and as she crumbled to the floor I heard children inside crying for their mommy.

Things had gotten a little out of hand.

I held Carmen's head with both hands as I ejaculated into her mouth. We were parked behind the movie theater after our date, giving me a lovely view of a dumpster lit by the piss-glow of the single streetlight.

That's amore.

This was our first sexual act. Carmen was one of those women who didn't want to be seen as a whore by fucking you too early in the relationship, so they sucked you off instead. I'd never been able to make sense of that, but I was glad to not have to mount this goliath. Plus, she gave great head. Fat girls have to compensate for their physical flaws in whatever ways they can.

It'd been a stressful day and the orgasm flushed me with endorphins, releasing some of the tension in my neck and shoulders. I hadn't heard anything about Vin—not from him or Pino or otherwise. When I'd exited the tenement building, I'd opted out of hunting for the missing Stewart Yakel, prioritizing fleeing the scene of the murders. I'd taken off in Vin's Lincoln, and at my apartment I removed all the clothes I was wearing—including sneakers, socks, and underwear—and double bagged them in Hefty bags. I showered, scrubbed out my fingernails, and shampooed the flecks of dried blood from my hair. I then drove the Lincoln to a construction site and discarded the Hefty bag in an open dumpster, took the Lincoln to the same Wal-Mart at which I'd stalked Seri, walked several blocks to a nearby bar, had a few drinks to create an alibi, and then called a cab to bring me home.

Stewart would tell the cops what really happened. Inconvenient but unavoidable. He could give a description of me. That wasn't my biggest concern. My fear was Vin might have called for that ambulance after all. It was stupid of me to have left him with his phone. If he got caught, he'd be grilled about who'd been with him and sooner or later the police would dangle a deal in front of that cinderblock head of his. If he didn't give them the name of the killer, he'd be tried for the murders himself. Old Vin would be desperate for any avenue to avoid doing a life jolt in MacDougall-Walker Correctional Institution. Unless he was stupid, he'd rat me out to the bulls. If our roles were reversed, that's what I would do.

Hopefully the son of a bitch had bled to death.

Carmen wiped her chins with the back of her hand as I put myself back into my pants and lit a cigarette. Few things are better than a smoke after a blowjob. The manly combo makes you feel like Charles Bronson. She whispered dirty nothings in my ear, the smell of cum on her breath, a stark contrast to Natalie's near puritanical prudishness. Carmen's ego was at banquet, hilariously believing a man as handsome and fit as myself would really be interested in a woman of her vile corpulence. Even chubby chasers would find her level of blubber macabre. Only the truly perverted would be aroused by such a creature, yet she believed I was really into her. Women are prone to the most bewildering delusions.

"Are you as good at cooking as you are pleasing a man?" I asked. "If so, I've hit the jackpot."

She gave a shrill laugh. With every date she became more boisterous, her true self poking out from behind the polished façade of first impressions. On top of being fat, she was loud and crass and foul-mouthed. A real top dog.

"You'll just have to come over for dinner now, won't you?" she said, taking the bait.

"Guess I will."

She tried to kiss me. I turned my head away. She'd just swallowed my load for Christ's sake.

"Oh, right," she said, realizing. "Sorry."

I patted her thigh. "Dinner would be great, Carm. Just call and let me know."

I'd purchased a pre-paid phone from Target, so I didn't have to give my name to an account. They called them *burners* and they were popular with drug dealers because they were untraceable. Carmen teased me because it was a flip phone, but otherwise didn't have any idea it was disposable. She found it odd that I didn't have any social media accounts, but I'd told her I was too old for that sort of thing, which made her laugh.

"Oh, Leo," she'd said. "You're one of a kind."

"*One suspect was taken into custody,*" the newswoman said.

I leaned in closer to the television set.

"*He was rushed to the hospital where he remains in critical condition.*"

I fell back into the couch cushions. I needed another drink. Needed several. As the newswoman detailed the shooting at Gil Yakel's a police sketch of the killer appeared on the screen.

"*. . . suspect is considered armed and dangerous . . .*"

I stared back at cartoon visage of myself. The head seemed too round, the face wooden and lifeless. A piss-poor likeness if you asked me.

"*. . . police are asking anyone with information to . . .*"

A knock at my front door startled me. It was past midnight. I walked with hushed footsteps to my bedroom and slid the .38 snub nosed from its hiding place. I approached the door with the hammer cocked. If it were the police, they probably would have announced themselves by now or battered their way inside. If Stewart Yakel had somehow tracked me down, he'd better have brought backup; otherwise he'd just be selling wolf tickets, as we say in the joint. No matter who was at my door, I knew I wouldn't want to see them.

"Open up, Jackie," Pino said.

He must have seen my shadow in the peephole. I lowered the hammer on the revolver, tucked it into my jeans, and opened the door. Pino stood there with a grayed scowl. He was aging faster than a U.S.

president. He wore a paisley shirt that made him look like the wallpaper in a fag bar. One of his meathead flunkies was with him, a real Bluto guinea dressed in Johnny Cash black. I let them in.

"Get you a drink?" I asked.

Pino's grimace deepened. "No. We need to talk."

I led them into the kitchen where I poured myself straight bourbon. I looked to Bluto. "How 'bout you, Sasquatch? Fancy a beverage?"

Bluto shook his head. "I'm good."

"Jeez. Make a guy drink alone—"

"You were there, weren't you?" Pino said, more statement than question.

"Where's that, Pino?"

"Don't get cute with me. I'm in no fucking mood. Vin's in a coma, fighting sepsis at Saint Francis."

Good, I thought, *at least he hasn't had a chance to talk yet.*

Better yet, I no longer had to worry that the only other person who knew about the upcoming hit on Seri might spill the beans.

"The kike he was collecting on is dead and so are two others," Pino said. "All of 'em shot to shit. And the one that got out alive is singing, telling the cops far more than they ought to know. This is very bad, Jackie. Very fuckin' bad."

"Yeah," I said, noncommittal.

"I told you not to get fuckin' cute! You and Vin have been doing a lot of work together lately and that police sketch bears a striking resemblance."

"Jesus . . . you really think so?"

"So you're admitting it was you?" Again more of a statement.

Here goes. "He needed a hand."

"A hand?"

I explained all that had happened. No sense lying to him. Don't bite the hand that feeds and all that. If he was going to unleash Bluto on me as punishment for these homicidal blunders, there was little I could do about it. I just had to hope all our years working together would buy me some leniency.

When I finished telling Pino how the shakedown spiraled into carnage, he reached for the bourbon and poured himself one.

"Mother Mary on the cross," he grumbled, taking a drink. "This is no good, Jackie."

"I agree. If Vin wakes up the bulls are gonna want answers."

He put up one hand. "Don't worry. Vin's no squealer."

This lessened my worry, but didn't wipe it out completely.

"My concern is the one that got away," Pino said. "His old man had been dealing with us a lotta years. He knew a few things about our operation—compromising things. Who knows how much he told the kid." He refocused his frustration on me. "Why the fuck didn't you call me the moment you got outta there, Jackie? I mean, Jesus H. Christ."

"Guess I figured it'd be better if you didn't know. In case someone came asking about it, you wouldn't have to lie. You'd clear a poly."

It was a convincing enough bullshit story. My actual motivation had been to completely remove myself from the crime. I'd killed Gil and the woman so as to leave no witnesses. If I filled anyone in on my involvement, those deaths would essentially be in vain. You can't confide in anyone about committing homicide. When it comes to murder, trust is an idiot's prayer.

Pino changed the subject. "What about that other thing?"

"A work in progress. I'm very close."

"Taking your sweet time, aren't you?"

"C'mon, Pino. It has to be done right, for both our sakes."

He pursed his lips. "All right. I don't need details. Just tell me when the job is done. I could use some good news."

CHAPTER SEVEN

"**W**HERE'RE YOU GOING?" Natalie asked.

"Out."

She'd recently moved in with me. Initially I'd been against the idea, but again my desire to have a façade of normalcy won out. I'd even let her ancient cat come with her and allowed Natalie to do a little decorating to suit her tastes.

She huffed as I slipped into my dress shoes. "You've been going out a lot lately. Without me."

"It's a guy thing. We need our space. You can't expect me to completely change my life just because we live together."

Pouting, Natalie sat on the bed and crossed her arms. "Jackie, it's been weeks since we've gone out somewhere. I need to get out of the house too. Don't you like spending time with me?"

I kissed her on the forehead. "Don't be silly."

"That's not an answer."

She wasn't being standoffish; that wasn't her way. She was whining.

"Nat, of course I enjoy spending time with you. That's just not how I want to spend *all* of my time."

Silence. Her eyes grew wet. "Is there someone else?"

I finished tucking in my shirt. I lifted her chin until our eyes met and cleared a tear from her cheek with my finger. Then I backhanded her across the face. She fell onto the bed, gasping in shock. I'd never struck her before. Now that we'd gone domestic, it was time to lay down some firm ground rules. I grabbed her blouse, stretching it as I pulled her face close to mine.

"How dare you say that to me?" I said. "After all I've done for you!"

"Jackie, I'm sorry, I . . . "

I slapped her and her cheek turned my favorite color.

"Get this through your thick head," I said, pressing the point of my index finger against her nose. "You don't get to accuse me! Show a little respect, damn it! I'll go out whenever I please and do whatever I want. I don't owe you *any* explanations. Got it?"

She nodded repeatedly. I smacked her again.

"Say it!"

"You . . . can do what you want. You don't owe me explanations. I won't ever accuse you again, Jackie. I'm sorry . . . I just love you so much."

"Prove it."

I took out my already hard dick and made her suck me off while she was still crying and trembling, then decorated her face with cum. Then I left for my dinner date at Carmen's.

At first Carmen said she would send Seri to her dad's for the evening, but I manipulated her into letting me meet the girl, telling her it would be a good step forward for us. Love drunk, Carmen jumped at any opportunity to deepen our relationship.

When I arrived at the house it was Seri who answered the door. I hadn't seen her since that day at Wal-Mart and it made my legs grow weak. She was wearing a little blue dress with little white shoes and her hair looked as if she'd just visited the salon, her chocolate locks wavy like Christmas ribbons. I wondered what she'd look like with some eyeshadow and lipstick, like some JonBenét Ramsey pageantry nymphet. She gave me a shy, forced smile and I knew her mother had insisted she greet me at the door. If Seri recognized me from Wal-Mart, it didn't show.

"Hello, Mr. Leo," she said.

"Hi there, Seri."

She opened the door and stepped aside. Looking down at the girl, I suddenly remembered from some movie that vampires cannot enter your home unless invited. Carrying the bouquet I'd picked up at the grocery store, I squeezed through, brushing against Seri just slightly, and Carmen came thundering through the living room, palms going to her cheeks when she saw the roses.

"Oh, Leo, they're beautiful!"

"Beauties for my beauty," I said. I drew a box of candy from my pocket and handed it to Seri. "And sweets to the sweet."

She took the candy gingerly and gave me a weak, "Thank you."

There was no dining room, so we ate in the outdated kitchen—yellow floor tiles, wood paneling on the walls. A gigantic wooden fork and spoon hung from the wall. Chimes tinkled just outside the window. It takes a special breed of asshole for things like that.

Defying physics, Carmen seemed light on her feet as she flapped about, preparing everything like some even fatter Paula Dean. Something told me she didn't cook often. I envisioned meals in this house coming from a takeout window more often than a stove. There was wine from a box and a roll of paper towels as a centerpiece. She'd unscrewed two of three bulbs in the ceiling fan for mood lighting. I was somewhat surprised she used actual plates instead of plastic throwaways. As she finished making the meal I sat there with her daughter. I was tickled with elation, so close to the girl I could smell the lingering fragrance of her body wash. She'd made herself nice and clean for me.

"Are you looking forward to school starting?" I asked.

Seri shrugged. "I guess so."

"What grade will you be in now?"

"Sixth."

"That's right," Carmen said from behind the counter, her intrusion making me cringe inside. "Next year she'll be on to middle school already. My baby in junior high, can you believe it?"

I gave the pig a nod to satiate her and quickly returned my attention to Seri. She sat with hands folded in her lap, Alice in Wonderland sitting with the Mad Hatter. She was not prissy—they were too poor for that—but dainty, her lithe body so proper in her girlishness. The asinine babble of childhood was gone, leaving the smallest of ladies, like the core of a nesting doll. She wasn't puerile, but premature. Not nonsensical, but bashfully serious. Her in-progress transmogrification was a delight to witness.

"I appreciate you dressing so nice for me," I told her.

She blushed, tucking her head.

"Shorts and jeans are fine for girls," I said, "but dresses are for young ladies."

Silence. She fidgeted.

I dared to touch the shoulder strap of her dress. "Is blue your favorite color?"

"I dunno," she said, smiling awkwardly.

"I'll bet you look pretty in pink."

Carmen put the roses in a vase and placed them on the table. I moved it aside so not to block my view of even an inch of Seri Davidson. Sesame chicken and asparagus with sautéed mushrooms was served, all of it bland to the point of flavorless. I wasn't even hungry but slurped it up like a starved prisoner, knowing it would please Carmen to feed her man. It was vital to keep her happy. She seemed not only joyous, but proud.

"Leo is a successful man," she told Seri. "He takes your Mom to nice restaurants. Much nicer than Applebee's."

Carmen giggled at her own joke. Was she actually bragging about me to her daughter? Wasn't it usually the other way around, parents boasting to their guest about their precious little crotch goblins?

"Don't you think he's handsome?" she asked Seri.

My breath stopped in my chest, eyes burning into Seri as I awaited her answer.

The girl turned the color of strawberries. "Mom!"

"It's okay," Carmen said. "It's a nice compliment to give a man."

I almost concurred but didn't want to force the girl to say something she might not mean. As we ate, Carmen did most of the talking, yammering on about whatever stupid bullshit. I managed to reciprocate though my mind was lost in a reverie of the freakish and fantastic. I talked to Seri most of all, knowing my interest in her would be taken in a positive way by her mother. It would show I was invested in our relationship, when in reality I was succumbing to an obsession I had yet to fully understand.

Knowing why I was really here made Seri's impishness all the more alluring. Every blush and tucking of her head, every aversion from my gaze, every quiet, forced reply. It was easy to imagine that somehow, deep inside, she knew I was planning to take her life.

Carmen did the dishes as Seri and I retired to the living room. She sat on the sofa primly, her knees together, feet making an arrowhead. I thought of how Chinese women did foot-binding to make their feet look the way they had when they were eleven, even going so far as to have them broken so they could be bound flat against the soles. The concept excited me.

"So what do you like to do, Seri?"

"What do you mean?"

"What are your hobbies? How do you pass these long summer days when your mom is at work?"

"Um . . . I guess I like to go roller-skating."

"Really? That's interesting. You go to a rink?"

"Sometimes. Most of the time I just go to the park. There's a mile track there for runners I can use."

"Right," I said. I remembered passing the park on my way to and from the house. "You know, I actually ice-skated when I was a kid."

This brought a genuine smile out of her. "You did?"

"Sure. Don't laugh now."

She sucked in her lips to suppress a giggle.

"Hey now, I wasn't going to be a figure skater," I said. "I wanted to play hockey. But hey, skates are skates. Maybe we could all go roller-skating at a rink sometime soon. My treat."

She shrugged, still smiling. "Okay."

Carmen sashayed her fat fucking ass into the living room. My bowels churned at her intrusion.

"Oh, I don't think I can do any roller-skating," she said. "Not with my knees."

But the truth was she'd be out of breath in two minutes, if the wheels could even hold her. We all talked for a while and before I knew it Carmen was ushering off her daughter to bed. My heart sank.

"It's only ten," I said.

"And she's only eleven." The cow gave me a wink. "Besides, it's grown up time."

In a moment of stupidity, I thought she might have Seri give Uncle Leo a kiss goodnight. But of course not. The girl just gave me a wave and disappeared into the bathroom before going off to bed. I imagined the foam of toothpaste dribbling from the corners of her mouth, all creamy and white.

The kid in bed, Carmen and I snorted coke. I'd just bought a fresh bag from Max Marino—amongst other things. Carmen found a movie on Netflix I knew we wouldn't really be watching. She wanted to make out.

AND THE DEVIL CRIED

Once she was confident Seri was asleep, we went to the master bedroom and to my gulping horror Carmen began to disrobe. Rolls of protoplasm awaited me. At least fat girls have big tits. And this one wanted to take it in that leviathan of an ass.

Afterward she smoked a joint in bed while I puffed a cigarette. It was queen-sized, hardly big enough for both of us.

"Sorry," she said, "But you really shouldn't stay the night. I want you to, but it might not be the best thing for Seri to see you here in the morning."

My muscles quivered as that familiar, evil heat slithered through.

"Carm," I said. "It's late and—"

She put her finger to my lips and shushed me. "Please, Leo. It's just not time for that yet."

I'd been wondering about tranquilizers for Carmen. I had a sudden vision of her rumbling across an African plain on all fours as I fired darts at her.

"Okay," I said. "I understand."

Still we lay there, Carmen with her head on my chest. Once she began to snore, I slid out from under her and got dressed. I turned off the light, leaving her to hibernate, and moved down the hall on the balls of my feet like a cat burglar in a cartoon. I opened Seri's door slowly, the wood dragging across the carpet in a whisper. A *The Little Mermaid* nightlight gave the room a pinkish glow, throwing my shadow on the wall. Though she seemed a little old for that sort of thing, I liked seeing it. It was all that stood between her and the darkness I could cast.

Seri slept on her side. The room was warm from the summer night and no breeze came through the open window, so the covers were off her. She was dressed in only an oversized t-shirt. I figured it belonged to her daddy, giving her a way to cling to him when he wasn't around. Her cherub cheeks looked rouged but it wasn't makeup, only her fair skin responding to the peace of unconsciousness.

I loomed over her. Running one finger from her jaw down to her breastbone, I caressed the elegant neck, so small I could choke her with one hand.

Suddenly I heard Carmen's words in my head. "It's just not time for that yet."

Allowing myself just one more indulgence, I lifted the hem of Seri's shirt to glimpse her panties. The little bitch had worn pink for me. Pink with a little bow at the waistline, right below her belly button. White butterflies danced upon the underwear and I imagined smacking them all into smears of death. I released the shirt and walked out.

I bit at my thumbnails the entire way home. The stove clock told me it was past midnight. Natalie had left the light in the living room on for me. I turned on the bedside lamp when I came into the bedroom. She was still asleep and had a black eye. Once I was in bed, she scooted over to me and rested her head on my chest just as Carmen had an hour ago. She ran her palm up and down my belly, kissed my cheek, and said nothing.

I slept like a fucking baby.

In the morning, Natalie apologized to me for yesterday's behavior and I had her repent by sucking me off again, particularly because I hadn't washed since fucking Carmen in the ass. Natalie made no objections despite what horror she may have tasted.

Instead of letting her finish, I decided to make love to her, literally throwing her a bone. If you want to break a woman, it can't be nothing but abuse. You always have to leave them teetering between love and a loss of love—between joy and terror, pleasure and pain.

"You know I don't like to hurt you," I said, running my fingers through her hair. "It makes me sick to have to do it."

She kissed me. "I'm sorry for putting you in that position, Jackie."

"Oh, Natalie," I said, smiling like a new groom. "What am I gonna do with you?"

She actually giggled and we kissed again.

People deserve every bad thing that happens to them.

***

It's not easy to rent a place when you've been to prison. Landlords do background checks and reserve the right to deny your application based on a felony conviction. I doubted I'd be successful if I attempted a court order to seal my record.

So I started looking to buy. Banks might be weary to give a loan to an ex-con, but on paper I had a full-time job. I was rehabilitated and a free man with a six-grand deposit in hand. After two denials, I reached out to the FHA, a federally funded organization that insures loans for former felons. This made lenders more at ease and I was able to purchase a single-story house near the Farmington River with enough surrounding woods to satisfy my need for privacy.

I didn't tell anyone about the place, including Natalie.

I wasn't planning to move into it yet.

I was alone in the apartment when Hugh Autry made a surprise visit, one of the conditions of my parole. The hillbilly shuffled his feet as he came in. The back of his shirt was stained with sweat and his eyes were a touch bloodshot.

A drunk, I thought, *totally hung over*.

He carried a clipboard like some high school gym teacher.

"Well now," he said, looking at the furniture. "Where'd you get all this fancy stuff?"

"It's my girlfriend's. She moved in."

"Girlfriend?" he asked, eyebrows raised. "You didn't tell me you had a girlfriend."

"Didn't realize it was something I had to report."

He smirked. "You know, I stopped into Giuseppe's a few times this week. Wouldn't you know it, you just happened to not be there each time."

"I've been doing a lot of prep work in the early mornings before we open. Making roast beef and cold case items, that sort of thing."

"Uh huh. Well, I'll be checking in there this week and I better see you there, capisce?"

Autry worked his way through the apartment, tapping his pen against the clipboard, taking things in. He didn't ask permission, just rooted through my bathroom, opening cabinets and pulling back the shower curtain. He even lifted the toilet tank lid. I followed him to the bedroom, fists aching to hammer his kidneys. He opened the dresser drawers, looking for drugs or anything else he could drag me back to Hell over. If he did, he would probably jizz in his pants.

I purposely kept the place clean. All my treasures were hidden in the air vents: the two grand I'd swiped from Gil Yakel, along with his jewelry and stamp collection; Vin's .22 caliber; my snubnosed revolver and shoulder holster; a small baggie of cocaine for the days after my drug tests; and another two baggies of drugs for a special occasion.

When Autry came to the drawer containing Natalie's underwear, his beer gut jiggled as he snickered under his breath. He used his pen to lift a pink lingerie top.

"Ooh, la la," he said in his dumbass southern drawl.

He was baiting me, trying to boil my blood so I'd do something drastic, proving I wasn't as rehabilitated as I presented myself to be. Typical pig. They get a little power and immediately start pissing on everybody's shoes. Parole officers are like any other breed of lawman in that they live to see you fail. The last thing they want is an absence of crime. A lack of criminals to beat down wouldn't just take their paycheck away, it would take away all their fun. Cruelty is the only thing that brings joy to their black fucking hearts. They want people to hurt so they can slurp their tears, wolves lapping blood from a fresh kill. Because if they hurt others enough their victim's souls might corrode as much as theirs had.

I was twenty-six when I was discharged from the

army. Eight years of assassinating ragheads and raping their women had left me in a deranged mental state. Coming back to America was a paralyzing shock. I was still conditioned to war and found myself peeking around corners before I'd change aisles in the grocery store, or spinning around sharply when anyone strolled up behind me. Too fucked up for a regular job, I began blowing through my savings just to pay the bills, and when that well ran dry I had a slow but steady nervous breakdown. In a manic state fueled by a hellish combination of depression and drugs, I bought a Halloween mask and took my pump-action shotgun to the neighborhood bank. Less than two hours later, I was in the back of a police cruiser. One of the tellers had given me a bundle of cash rigged with a tracking device.

Now, after over six years of a seven-year sentence served, I was free, and pigs like Hugh Autry just couldn't stand that. I'd hurt no one in the bank robbery, but in his eyes it did nothing to lessen my insult to the American tradition of suckers working long hours for shitty pay, making the rich richer by toiling under the weight of the machine. The pride of the American work ethic is the least funny of all jokes. To assholes like Autry, a man's simple act of desperation is a capital offense. I may not have deserved a lethal injection, but I sure as shit shouldn't find any semblance of happiness.

As he sifted through my girlfriend's panties, I imagined Autry's wife—basically Carmen, only with a less lovely face and twice as shrill, her husband's balls tucked in her purse between a used Kleenex and a spare tampon. When he'd finished invading Natalie's privacy, we returned to the kitchen, the redneck writing on his clipboard all the way.

"Keep your nose clean, Jackie," Autry said before leaving.

On principal, I snorted a line as soon as he'd gone.

The three of us went to the skating rink on Saturday.

True to her word, Carmen remained on the sidelines, sitting at a table with a bag of popcorn, watching Seri and I roller-skate. I pretended to be a rusty just so Seri would hold my hand. Her soft flesh made mine shiver. We spun around a curve, and I put my palm to the small of her back. I deliberately bumped hips with her, making it look like an accident, then put my hands on her waist so she wouldn't fall. She didn't object to my touching and neither did her mother. Carmen's trust in me was as blind, deaf, and dumb as Helen fucking Keller.

Life is either a daring adventure, or nothing.

Keller had said that—and I was following her advice.

I took Seri's hands and we went into a spin. The disco ball bounced a rainbow of lights across her, illuminating her laughing face. She was warming up to me. K.C. and the Sunshine Band sang from the speakers, telling us to do a little dance, make a little love. Seri's hair danced about as if underwater and I thought of the mermaid nightlight in her bedroom and how it had shone upon her panties. I wondered if she had pink ones on right now, the same lovely color of what lay beneath. My precious prey. My seraph. My oblivious girl on the threshold of dying.

I bought her Junior Mints and gave her quarters for the video games. We played Galaga and she teased me about how old it was. I let her beat me in Skee-Ball and gave her my tickets. All in all, an excellent afternoon. I knew it was risky for me to be seen with these two in public. We can't deprive ourselves of all of life's simple pleasures, though.

As Seri went to cash in her tickets for a prize, Carmen told me she was in love with me. She invited me back to the house, but I told her I'd brought office work home to get a head start on a tough week. I arrived at the apartment to find the pots and dishes from breakfast still in the sink. So when Natalie got home from work I beat her, fantasizing about Seri as my knuckles drew blood.

Giuseppe pulled me aside as I put on my deli apron.

"Jackie boy," he said. "This thing with Natalie. It's no good."

"What're you talking about?"

He nodded in her direction. She was helping a customer, oblivious to us.

"Her face, Jackie. She's got a black eye again. Bruises. The first time, she tell me she walked into a door. Now she say she fell and hit her head on the sink. But I'm no fool."

"With all due respect, Giuseppe, you should mind your own business."

He put up his hands, a passive gesture. "I no mean

to pry. Love is . . . complicated. But I can't have her looking like this. It upsets the customers. They worry. Get suspicious."

Because I still needed this job as a front, I didn't give Giuseppe a taste of the beatings he was complaining about. He also had a point. If the wrong person found out I was punching around my woman, it might get back to Hugh Autry. For all I knew, domestic violence was a parole violation.

"All right," I said. "I'll take care of it."

He patted my shoulder. "You're a good boy, Jackie. One day you marry Natalie and she'll become a housewife. Then you can do with her whatever. Not for nothin', but a man has a right to keep his wife in line."

I worked the deli counter a few hours, a relaxing reprieve from my usual work of going all over town to rattle people for their loan payments. It was a mellow day. There'd been no police developments in the death of Gil Yakel, his son Donald, or twenty-nine-year-old Hannah Johnston, the woman I'd killed in the hall. Vin remained in a coma. From what I'd heard he was not expected to come out of it. I wondered who had his power of attorney. He was divorced and I wasn't sure if he had grown children, so I just sent flowers to the hospital. Of course I couldn't visit; nor would I wish to even if I weren't involved in the crime that had landed him there. The flowers were simply for appearances, a showing of respect that would keep Pino from getting pissed off.

I hoped Hugh Autry would stop in and catch me working, but even though I stayed through the lunch rush he didn't show. Cocksucker wanted to keep me stressed about it. Rather than let him take up residence in my mind, I focused on thoughts of Seri and the plan I was forming.

Playtime was over.

CHAPTER EIGHT

AFTER CHECKING MULTIPLE times throughout the week, I finally caught Seri at the park. She was skating around the mile track, pigtails bobbing on her shoulders, nimble legs pumping. I scanned the area. A Little League game was in progress. Parents cheering their talentless tikes. A pair of teenage boys with long hair sat on the swings, probably having just smoked a joint in the woods. A young mother stood in a sandpit, watching her child play on a rocking horse on a spring. The kid looked constipated.

But Seri was alone. She must have skated from the house. I wondered if Carmen knew she was here. She allowed Seri to go to the park by herself—unlike most parents these days—but if Carmen was at work, would Seri have to call and let her know every time she was going to set foot out of the house? Judging by what I'd seen of their relationship, I doubted it. Carmen was a caring mother, but also a lax one, and proud Seri was maturing.

I got out of my Dodge Charger and started toward the track. The teenage boys watched me until I stared back—*hard*. The punks were unaware that at any moment I could subtly draw my revolver, march them to the bathroom building, and rape the little shits just to teach them a lesson. I'd certainly done it in prison. In the joint, I'd have used these two sweethearts as currency. So young and tender.

At the track, I watched my girl flow like water, the breeze at her back as if angels were bracing her. How many times had I fucked Carmen in missionary position so I could see her face, just because it was so much like her daughter's? How many times had I fucked Natalie while thinking of Seri as I felt her tiny breasts, so like those of a blossoming girl? I'd even bought a tabletop disco ball for the bedroom to recreate the rink and roller-skates for Natalie to wear in bed. She found it odd but didn't object. She was learning. What I found strange, however, was during these sexual transgressions I didn't exactly fantasize I was fucking Seri—even though I'd thought that's what I'd wanted. Instead, my brain flooded with memories of her doing the simplest things—sitting with her knees together or pounding the buttons on the Galaga machine or sipping Dr. Pepper from a straw. All my imagination cooked up were flashes of the many ways I could hurt her. Her face became black and blue then—like Natalie's when I was in a mood—and her nose burst with blood just as Stewart Yakel's had when I'd knocked him to the floor. Then, in my fantasized moment of murder, I would ejaculate. That I often did so inside the mother of the child I was plotting to kill made it all the sweeter.

Seri came around the curve. I waved her down. She smiled when she saw me. The nervous tension she'd once felt around me had dissipated. I was mom's boyfriend now. Maybe she wasn't ready for a stepdad, but she didn't dislike having me in her life.

She was mature enough to know her mother's happiness was just as important as her own.

"Leo," she said, coming to a slow halt. "What're you doing here?"

"Hey, Seri. Your mother asked me to pick you up."

She gave me a quizzical look. "She did? What for? Is everything okay?"

"Things'll be fine. I'll explain in the car. C'mon, we need to get going."

It was a risky bluff. Carmen had gotten her daughter a phone for emergencies. All Seri had to do was shoot Mommy a text to find out I was lying. But I was already taking a much more dangerous gamble, so what was one more? I took her hand. When she didn't pull away, I knew I had her.

"But where're we going?" she asked.

I guided her down the concrete pathway toward the parking lot so she wouldn't have to stop and take off her skates. The less time she had to think about this, the better.

"It's a surprise," I said. And boy, was it ever.

"I don't understand."

"If you did, it would ruin the surprise, silly. Now c'mon, would ya? We don't wanna be late."

I chuckled, my smile beaming all for her. The desire to get us out of there was ardent. I watched everything at once in my peripherals, every sense acute, and kept Seri close. The union of our locked hands was warm and clammy, as exhilarating as the joining of genitals. I opened the passenger door of the Charger and she got inside. She bent over in the seat and my heart leapt into my throat, fearing she was going for her phone.

She was only untying her skates.

"I don't have my sneakers," she said as I started the car.

"You won't need them."

Her brow furrowed. "Are we going to a pool party or something?"

I pointed to the bottle of Dr. Pepper in the cup holder. "It's hot out there. Have a drink. I brought this for you."

"Thanks." She took a long drink. "Are we going to The Sound? I keep telling Mom I want to go to the beach. Is that it?"

I gave her a sly look but said nothing.

"Hope she brought my bathing suit."

I pictured her in a bikini and licked my lips. Seri drank her soda, her own lips moistening.

"How's your Dr. Pepper?" I asked.

She looked at it. "Actually, it tastes a little funny. Is this some new flavor?"

"I don't know."

"I'm so thirsty though. It's hot today. Thanks for getting it."

"My pleasure. Want some music?"

I didn't wait for a reply. Turning on the stereo, I selected the playlist I'd created just for this moment. The jovial disco of K.C. and The Sunshine Band's "Get Down Tonight" rose from the speakers like a siren song, calling each of us to our destiny. I kept glancing at Seri, waiting for any sign of recognition.

Finally I had to ask. "Remember this one?"

She gazed at the stereo's face, as if that would help her recognize it.

She shrugged. "I don't think so."

The evil heat began to stir. My skin became mottled, hairs standing at attention.

"Are you serious?" I asked.

Again she shrugged. "I don't really like oldies."

There was a sudden pounding in my ears, drowning out the music, and I had to suppress a guttural roar.

"Seri," I said. "Don't you remember the skating rink?"

Her eyes darted, the first sign of worry. "Yeah . . . "

"This is it!" I said, pointing at the stereo. "This is *our song*!"

Silence. The girl put her hands to her belly, shoulders forward, making her appear smaller. Her hair created a curtain for her to hide behind and I had to resist the urge to reach out and shake her, to demand she acknowledge our special memory. But it was all too clear I'd made her uneasy, perhaps even scared.

I pulled onto the freeway.

"Leo?" she said.

My tone was firm. "What?"

"I need to call my mom real quick." She reached into the pocket of her shorts. "Can you just turn down the music for just a se—"

I slapped the phone from her hand. It fell to the floorboards. Seri gasped, eyes darting. I could almost feel the tingling inside her right now, almost smell the first bead of terror-sweat forming at the base of her spine. An erection pulsed against my slacks.

"Wha . . . what's," Seri said. "Leo?"

"You need to chill out, Seri."

She glanced at her phone on the floor.

"Leave it," I said. "Just drink your soda."

She hung her head, hiding behind that lovely brunette hair again. "Um . . . Leo? Can you take me home, please?"

I gripped the wheel harder. "What? And miss the surprise?"

She didn't reply. When I looked at her again, she was trembling.

"Leo . . . I just wanna go home. Please? I . . . I, um . . . don't feel good."

"Finish your drink. It'll settle your stomach."

She looked at the soda, then at me, and in that glance I knew she'd figured it out. But she dared not say it. I stuck to the highway so there'd be no traffic lights, no chance for her to leap out of the car without hitting the pavement at seventy-five miles per hour. Tears rolled down Seri's cherub cheeks, the hints of pending young adulthood vanishing, fear devolving her back into a full-fledged child. She held her stomach.

"I'm gonna throw up," she whimpered.

"Then use the window."

She tried to hold it back but couldn't. A projectile of brown, chunky syrup burst from her mouth as she leaned out the window. She was really crying now.

"I want my mom . . . "

She flinched when I patted her head. I put my arm around her, pulling her into me like a loving boyfriend. She knew better than to resist. Her torso quivered in my grip.

"Seri?" I said. "Do you know what psychedelic mushrooms are?"

Silence as she trembled against me.

"People make tea out of them. It usually makes them throw up before they start hallucinating."

Silence. Trembling.

"How about PCP?" I asked. "You know what that is? When I was your age, they taught us all about drugs. It was part of this program they had called D.A.R.E. Do they still have that?"

No answer.

"If not, they really should," I said. "It's a shame to see a young girl like you doing drugs like those, especially at the same time."

PART TWO

HOME SWEET HOME

CHAPTER NINE

"**P**CP?" **MAX HAD ASKED.** "The fuck you want that for? Nobody takes that shit these days. It fucks you up too much."

I sipped my beer. "That's what I'm looking for."

"Jack, I don't mean 'fucks you up' in a good way. I took that shit at a party once and dude, I tripped harder than any acid you ever dreamed. A wicked bad trip too, lemme tell ya. I was paranoid to the point of panic. Made me crazy aggressive. I may not look like much, but I tossed some guy down the stairs and kicked the shit outta him just 'cause he was talkin' to my girl. And on PCP, ya crash hard. I was so anxious I had to isolate myself in my apartment for weeks." He took a drag on his cigarette, the rings under his eyes darker every day. "I've seen a guy punch a car to pieces on that stuff. Took four cops to pin him down and then he broke the cuffs. And he wasn't any bigger than my skinny ass. It was like seeing David Banner turn into the Hulk."

"I can handle it, Max."

"I'm just sayin'. People are even known to kill themselves."

Exactly, I'd thought.

Max told me he'd see what he could do. He had

the mushroom tea but getting PCP would involve reaching out to his local dealer. Later that night, Max met me at The Chimney, delivering my complete order.

"No matter what you do," he'd said. "Don't take this shit together. You'll go insane."

Seri's eyes were dilated and bloodshot, simultaneously. She looked around wildly as we pulled into the driveway, an animal cornered. She babbled under her breath in a schizophrenic panic. I wasn't worried she'd make a run for it now. I'd driven on the freeway long enough for the drugs to blast her mind to bits. Her nails sunk into the sleeve of my shirt as if she'd be sucked into space if she let go. Perhaps, in a way, she would be.

Though she was aware I'd poisoned her, she latched herself on to the only available adult; the one man who might help her through this. I touched her wrist. Her pulse pounded. Sweat slicked her hair to her skull.

I hit the remote and the garage door opened. As we pulled into the shadows, Seri panted like a hound. I had paper grocery bags in the house just in case, having anticipated the possibility she'd hyperventilate. The last thing I wanted was for her to pass out. I waited for the garage door to close before unlocking the car. Seri shrieked and clung to my arm, my little pet monkey.

"No! Don't leave me!"

"Relax," I said. "We're going inside."

I pulled free, went around to her side, and undid her seatbelt.

"Leo . . . " she said, "Leo . . . something's wrong . . . "

"Yes. It is."

I scooped her up like a man carrying his new bride across the threshold. Her delicate body quaked in my arms. I thought of a father cradling his newborn—the same flood of emotion washing over me, drowning me, taking me deeper into the black ocean of delirium.

We entered the house. Seri stared at its emptiness. "There's no stuff."

"No. Only downstairs."

I carried her to the kitchen and through the door, down the staircase and into the basement. It was cooler beneath the earth. My sweat chilled. I'd furnished the sepulcher with a cot, a small desk, wooden stool, and sofa chair. The only other things in the basement were the oil tank, furnace, and water heater. The latter had been an ideal place to setup the main camera with two more placed in the ceiling, one equipped with night vision. A set of barn doors led up to the backyard. I'd fortified it with steel bars on the inside and a hundred-pound cement slab placed on the outside. I'd outfitted the kitchen door at the top of the stairs with multiple deadbolts. There was only one window down here—too small for even a girl her size to squeeze through. I'd boarded it up anyway with a metal plank, screwing it into the concrete.

Slowly I put her down on the cot. She pulled the pillow to her chest as if it were a teddy bear. "Where are we?" she asked in a shaky voice. Her eyes were wild like she'd already been kept in isolation. "Where am I?"

I ran my hand over her head. "Where do you think, silly?"

She had no answer, only teeth that chattered the song of madness.

"You're home, Seri," I said. "Home sweet home."

The look of complete horror that flushed her face was astonishing. Never had I seen a look of such pure, unsuppressed fear, not even in a merciless prison or on a battlefield in a desert Hell. It was terror, anguish, and despair all boiled down into the most concentrated of all human pain.

I wanted to sing and dance and laugh and masturbate. Instead I stood there in awe.

"Please . . . " she said in a whimper trending toward squeal. "Please, Leo . . . "

"C'mon. You're a smart girl. You should know by now that's not my name."

She went even paler. "Please . . . sir . . . I want—"

"You want your mommy?"

She closed her eyes tight, nodded.

"You know, Seri. You should see the things Mommy lets me do to her. You wouldn't believe your eyes—wouldn't believe it was the same woman." I put my hand on her shoulder. She flinched and I squeezed tighter. "We never really know anyone, little girl. Never."

"I just want my mom . . . "

"Well, I hate to break it to you, but Mommy doesn't want you. That's why she gave you to me."

Seri shook her head. "No! No! No!"

"Well, you're right. I shouldn't say 'gave.' It was more like 'sold.' She *sold* you to me. Would you like to know for how much? Wanna know what you're worth?"

She couldn't answer. She was bawling in deep, grievous breaths.

"Okay. We can discuss that later." I stepped away from the cot, turning toward the staircase. "There's a box under your bed there. It has a flashlight, some reading material, and some new clothes. I suggest you use them all."

I started up the staircase. Seri jumped off the cot so quickly she fell on her knees, scraping them. Still hallucinating, she wobbled back to her feet, calling after me.

"That's not what they mean by *tripping on mushrooms*," I said. "Have a nice time. I'll be back. Eventually."

I reached the kitchen, shut the door in her panicked face, and bolted it up. I flicked the wall switch, turning off the light in the basement, letting the darkness swarm around my girl as she screamed and screamed and screamed.

CHAPTER TEN

CARMEN CALLED ME that night, hysterical. It was perfect timing. Natalie was at work, covering the night shift for someone who'd called out sick. I'd waited to destroy the burner phone just for this very call, knowing it'd be too good to miss.

"Leo," Carmen said, "I don't know what to do. Seri was gone when I came home. *Gone!* I thought she was just out with friends. Her roller-skates are missing and I figured she was rolling around the neighborhood."

She didn't even ask me if I'd seen her. Her idiot trust in me was astounding. But I knew the police would look into the new boyfriend. I'd never taken Carmen to my place for this very reason—well, that and the risk of Natalie and Carmen discovering each other—and had told her I worked at a bank in Stamford, a good hour south.

"Try to calm down," I said.

"I called the cops. They put out an Amber alert. To think my baby might be abdu—"

"Don't say that, Carm. I mean, maybe she is with a friend after all."

"She would've called." She sniffled in my ear. "I tried calling her a hundred times and it just goes to voicemail."

"Maybe she lost her phone."

"They're tracking it now. It last pinged in Springfield. *Massachusetts*, Leo. She went across the border!"

"We only know her phone went there, not her. Maybe it was stolen."

But she was blubbering again. "My Seri . . . my sweet little girl . . . "

I rubbed the erection pushing against my fly. Natalie would get fucked good tonight.

"Carm, I still think it's possible she's just with a friend." I resisted the laughter rising from my stomach. "We have to think positive."

Her breathing steadied. "Leo? Can you come over?"

I gave her a moment of silence. "Oh, Carm. I'm sorry, babe. I'd love to, but you know . . . "

"Know what?" Her voice wavered, confused.

"I've been meaning to talk to you."

I paused, waiting. The whale made no song.

"This *thing* between us," I said. "I just don't think it's been working."

Panicked breathing. "Wha . . . what? What?"

"I'm just not feeling it, ya know? I'm just not happy in our relationship, if you can even call it that. This may not be the best time, but . . . I want to break up."

Sobs. Sweet, arousing sobs. I unzipped my fly, spat in my hand, and began masturbating.

"I just need time to find myself," I said. "You understand."

"Not the *best time*?" she said, anger brewing. "Gee, *ya think*? You need to fucking *find yourself*! I'm trying to find *my daughter*, Leo!"

"Yes, well . . . best of luck."

"You selfish son of a bitch," she said. "How could you do this to me *now*? You heartless bastard!"

"Easy, Carm. No need for name-calling. I haven't called you a fat, disgusting porker."

She started screaming, unintelligible. I jerked off faster. In the corner, Natalie's cat watched me from his bed, curious.

"Someone needs to tell you," I said. "You're a bovine whore. Maybe if you spent more time with your daughter instead of snorting coke off my dick, she might not have run away."

"You fucking bastard!"

"Face it, Carm. She ran away from you."

"You miserable fuck!"

"Better than being a dead fuck. You just lay there like a beached whale when it gets thrown in ya."

As she bawled, I put the phone to my dick, furiously masturbating.

"What is that?" she said. "Are you . . . *Jesus, are you jacking off?*"

I grunted as I came, Carmen's shock and anguish the greatest aphrodisiac. Of course I wanted to fuck her one more time. Imagine the ecstasy of fucking her while I had her daughter in a makeshift prison, out of her mind on drugs. But Carmen wouldn't have been in the mood, not even as a distraction. Besides that, the cops were involved now. I didn't need them seeing my face.

"You're sick!" she said. "You're a horrible, horrible—"

"Maybe Seri's dead, Carm. What if she hitchhiked to get away from you and got used up like a lot lizard

114

at a truck stop, huh? Maybe her phone wasn't the only thing that was discarded."

Her sobs fell away, and a gruff voice came on the line.

"Who is this?" he said.

I only laughed.

"This is Lieutenant Gregory," he said. "Police department!"

Like that mattered or something.

"Who is this?" he asked. "What is your name, sir?"

I heard Carmen screaming in the background. "I think *he* did it! Leo has my baby!"

I would savor the sound always, like a song that sticks in your head but you like it right where it is. The powerless cop barked more demands and I hung up. I doubted they'd been recording or tracing, but it was possible.

After placing the phone in double Ziplock bags, I smashed it with a hammer and drove it to the Connecticut River. There I said goodbye to Carmen. Forever.

When Natalie got home, she claimed to be too tired to have sex, having worked a sixteen-hour day. I pushed her down onto the kitchen counter, pulled down her jeans, and forced my way into her, dry. Sometimes it seemed like her lessons would never end. I thought of Seri alone in the basement with only a flashlight and wondered if she'd looked at the newspaper clippings I left for her, the ones detailing her father's drunken manslaughter of Pino's son. I thought of Carmen falling to the floor in hysterics, gutted by grief. I shot my seed into my human receptacle. Afterward, she shuffled around the kitchen as she made me dinner and I stretched out on the sofa watching *The Simpsons*, drinking bourbon and laughing my ass off.

It'd been a productive day. I'd earned some me time.

Pino was smiling, a jack-o-lantern with a tan.

We were at his poolside table again, his favorite place of business. Though the family would never fully recover from their loss, they were doing their best to return to some semblance of "normal" life. Rosalie was in the kitchen making pasta sauce from scratch. Drea was sunbathing in a bikini—blue this time, unfortunately, but it was still a treat to see so much girl flesh. Rosalie brought us all fresh-squeezed lemonade, then scurried off into the house again.

"You tell her?" I asked Pino.

"Only that it was done. Not who took care of it."

I would have enjoyed her adulation and gratitude, but the less people who knew, the better. I hadn't even elaborated to Pino. He didn't know about my relationship with Carmen or the dates we'd gone on with Seri tagging along. All I'd told him was I'd taken care of it. The daughter of the man who'd killed his son was gone. Pino didn't want any details and it pleased me not to have to lie to him—though I would have if pressed. He didn't want to know how I'd killed the girl or if she'd suffered. He was content as long as Seri was dead.

Of course, she wasn't. Not yet. But fuck Pino.

He slid an envelope to me. "The amount we

agreed upon. Plus ten percent. You earned it. Most guys I know would've flinched. But not you, Jackie. You've got balls big enough for the NBA to dribble."

I slipped the envelope into my pocket without counting it. There was no need to with Pino. He was the most honest crook I knew.

Though the police sketch artist did a slightly better job this time, it was far from a recognizable likeness. Those sidewalk artists at Coney Island churn out better portraits. It didn't worry me.

What did give me concern was the photograph.

Carmen had not asked me to take any pictures. It was still early in our "relationship" for the obligatory, romantic selfie. And I'd made it clear I was against the social media slideshow, saying I disliked the contractual rules that make users forfeit their privacy so companies can sell your information. She'd not posted the picture on social media, but she'd taken one.

I stared at it on the local news show. Thank Christ it was from a distance. All you could see was a man holding a girl's hands as they spun around a roller rink. The rainbow-colored lights obscured the image, leaving the faces half in shadow, the eyes dark pockets like in a skull. Zooming in only further distorted the features.

It *could* be me. It could also be any guy with dark hair and a lean frame.

I bought a copy of the *Hartford Courant* at CVS. Front-page news. I also purchased Tootsie Rolls, more toilet paper, and a picture frame.

I'd filled the bucket halfway with water. It helped, but the corner still reeked of urine and feces. I placed the new bundle of toilet paper beside the remaining ones.

Seri was still in the clothes she'd been wearing at the park. I glowered.

"You need to change outfits," I said.

The girl was pale, a ghost of herself. "What?"

She'd survived a night of psychedelic terror, but the aftereffects lingered. Her memory was fuzzy. Her words dragged.

"The clothes in the box. Put 'em on."

Her eyes darted side to side. "I don't wanna do that. Not with you here."

"I'll turn around."

Silence.

"Do it or you don't eat."

I had to help her off the cot. Her movements reflected queasiness and confusion. True to my word, I turned around and let her change in privacy.

"Okay," she said when finished.

I turned back. My mouth went agape at the sight of her. Little pink dress. White petticoat beneath. Bobby socks. Buckle shoes. And though I could not see them, I knew the panties were as pink as newly forming roses. My perfect little doll.

No. Not perfect.

"Forgetting something?" I asked.

Seri stared at me. I pointed to the box. She drew the headband from it, one with a pink bow at the top, and pulled it over her forehead, sliding her hair back.

AND THE DEVIL CRIED

My skin tingled as if crackling with static electricity. Some of her slouching was due to the narcotics, but we would still have to work on her posture. The drugs had also taken a toll on her cherub face. There were bags under her eyes more appropriate to an older woman. Her lips were chapped, some parts bright red from where, addled by nerves, she chewed the top layer of skin off.

I approached her. She was too broken to pull away. I ran my hand over one of her cheeks and gave her a little bop on the nose with my fingertip.

"Boop."

I took the full-sized Tootsie Roll from my pocket and handed it to her. She looked at it like it was a turd.

"What do we say?" I asked.

She managed a pathetic, "Thank you."

I motioned for her to sit on the cot and planted myself in the sofa chair, watching her munch on the candy. The day before I'd left her only with a gallon of bottled water and three boxes of Milk Duds.

Sweets to the sweet.

"I spoke to your mother last night," I said.

Seri looked up, suddenly wide-awake. "Mom?"

I crossed one leg over the other, bobbing one dangling foot. "She was a bit drunk when she called. She's been celebrating her new freedom, see? I mean, you can't blame her. She doesn't have to cook for you or take you to school or worry about your grades. She doesn't have to pay doctor's bills and buy you new clothes at Wal-Mart. But most of all she's excited for all the free time. Said she can live her life again without you dragging her down."

"No . . . " Seri said. "No, she didn't say that."

119

"She wanted me to come over and party with her. Told me she had some coke and—oh, sorry. You do know she does cocaine, right?"

Seri couldn't look at me. "No."

"You mean *No* as in you didn't know? Or *No* you refuse to believe me?"

She shook her head.

I chuckled. "The only thing she likes more than getting high is taking new men to bed. Has she talked to you about sex yet, Seri?"

I watched with bated breath as she drew her knees together. That this was her instinct gave me a rush of power.

"She'll have a lot more time for sex without you moping around," I said. "One of the reasons she wanted me to come over was to join her and three other men in, well . . . perhaps I'll explain when you're older."

She shook her head, flushing with vehemence. The remainder of the Tootsie Roll was hurled at my feet. Is there anything more adorable than a little girl pushed to the point of rage?

"You're lying!" she said.

"Two of those men are black too. How'd you like a nigger for a new dad?"

"You're just a big liar!"

I snickered, having myself a gay old time. "I see. Well, do newspapers lie, Seri?"

In an instant she went from hellfire furious to cold as a corpse.

"You did do the homework I left for you, right?" I asked. She didn't answer. "Sure you did. I can tell. Did you know your daddy was a murderer? That he likes to run over children your age? Why do you suppose that is?"

She hung her head, using her long hair to hide her tears. "Stop . . . "

"I have a theory. See, I think he was just as sick and tired of you as your mother was. That's why he left you two in the first place, right? But that wasn't enough. You made him hate kids so much he had to murder one."

Seri clutched her chest as if her heart were exploding and collapsed on the cot with her back to me, bawling.

"Your mom told me it was all your fault," I said. "Because of you, she lost her husband, the love of her life. Now your dad is gonna lose his freedom and spend the rest of his life in prison. All thanks to you, Seri."

I felt myself getting hard. It had nothing to do with sexual desire—at least not of the physical kind. It was the misery that seduced me, the torture of this living nightmare I had thrust Seri into. It was enough to make the devil cry.

"If you weren't so selfish," I said, "you'd see why she was so eager to get rid of you."

She was howling now. No use trying to talk to her. Not being a total savage, I took the toilet bucket out to the woods to dump it, sprayed it out, and brought it back to the basement. I placed the other two Tootsie Rolls on the desk, then drew the small picture frame from the coat of my blazer and situated it at the top.

The paper photo captured us in time—me and my Seri, eternally spinning in magic.

I bolted the door behind me and turned off the lights.

CHAPTER ELEVEN

WHEN PEOPLE FIND out you've been to prison, they jump to the conclusion that you had a bad childhood. That's not always the case. My parents were never cruel to me. I never watched my father beat my mother the way I ended up beating all my women; and men, for that matter. My mother didn't bring strange men home at night and my father wasn't a chronically unemployed drunk. He taught high school history and during the summer worked with my uncle building houses. My mother had a part-time job at a nail salon and spent the rest of her time as a homemaker. We were a middle-class family, and my folks took good care of Noah and me.

My brother was seven and a half years older than I was. My parents had always wanted more than one child but had put off having a second until they were financially stable. It was a good thing their money situation improved, otherwise a retard was the only child they ever would have had.

Noah wasn't full-blown retarded. He didn't have distorted features or walk crookedly or drool on himself. To look at him, you'd think he was a normal boy. But then he'd open his mouth and his mental slowness would become obvious. I was Mom and

Dad's second chance after this botched attempt at creating life.

As a child I thought my parents gave Noah special treatment because he was the oldest, causing me to despise him from an early age. That he could be Mommy's favorite instead of me was more than I could stand. As I grew older, however, I realized Noah was not so much a golden boy, but a burden. He was given special treatment because he needed it. He was cognizant enough to eat and bathe on his own, and collected carts at the grocery store, but required near constant assistance.

Though he had a warm, loving disposition, he was also very simple. My parents would be stuck with him *forever*.

Once that became clear to me, I didn't loathe my brother anymore. At least, not at first. My resentment toward him resurged when I grew old enough to be designated a caregiver, too. By the age of thirteen I was given the responsibility of babysitting him while my parents worked. I didn't even get paid for it. It was just another one of my chores. Of course, Noah, in all his delusions about being the big brother, thought it was he who was watching me—and *that* just left me all the more irritated with the moron. I was reaching an age where social interaction and popularity was everything, and here I was stuck with a two-hundred-pound anchor who nagged me to watch *The Never-Ending Story* enough times to justify its title.

Noah thought of me as his best friend. My actual best friend was Sonny Tipton.

Sonny came over to our house often. We'd met in the seventh grade and while I cannot remember how we'd initially bonded I do remember why I liked having him come over all the time. Sonny loved movies and his single, carefree mother let him watch whatever he wanted. We were both twelve when he introduced me to R-rated movies, which included not just violence but sex scenes with nudity. When we played, Sonny liked to recreate the scenes from his favorite movies, and he always portrayed the female characters, which I liked because I got to be all the tough guys.

We called it "acting."

One afternoon we were acting *The Terminator* and he initiated the scene where Sarah Conner is having sex with the hero, Kyle Reese. Actress Linda Hamilton played Sarah in the movie. Hers were the first bare breasts I'd ever seen. In the gray shadows of Sonny's room, we lay upon the bed, both of us shirtless, and I dry humped Sonny until I came in my pants. After that, we stuck to reenacting sex scenes from movies, including the rape scenes from *I Spit On Your Grave* and *The Accused*.

The first time Sonny jacked me off was also the first night I babysat Noah. I put on *The Never-Ending Story* for him. He was content on the couch with his Doritos and security blanket. Sonny had brought over a copy of *The Lost Boys*, thinking it'd be hilarious to put that movie on for Noah instead, but I refused.

"He'll just cry all night," I said. "Even some of the scenes in *The Never-Ending Story* make him shut his eyes and he's seen it a million times."

My friend balked. "Fine. You're such a wuss, Jack."

"Am not."

"Oh yeah?" he said. "Well, let's see ya prove it."

He led me to my bedroom, and we sat on the floor, face to face.

"I've got something cool to show you," he said, smirking. "But I don't think you'll do it. Wuss."

"Bullshit. I will too."

"Nuh uh. I'll have to dare you."

"Then dare me."

His smile grew. "I double-dog dare you."

But he didn't say what the dare was, insisting he'd just have to show me. Initiating our favorite scene from *The Terminator*, we undressed to our shorts, which we'd always kept on while humping. But this time Sonny reached for my erection as it pressed against him. Sudden fear washed over me. Someone else was actually touching my dick—and it was another boy. I snatched his wrist and moved his hand away.

"See," he said. "I knew you'd chicken out."

My voice quivered. "I'm not a faggot."

His laugh was forced. "It's just a game, Jack, remember? We're *acting*."

Slowly, cautiously, he put his hand between our crotches again, his palm facing me. I pressed against it, humping again, and soon Sonny had gripped me over my shorts. In the scene in *The Terminator*, Sarah Conner gets on top of Kyle Reese, so Sonny straddled me, took my penis out of my shorts, and finished me off.

I was shaking when I went to the bathroom to clean myself up. A harrowing shame was already beginning to fester. Yet, at the same time, I was exhilarated. When it came to sex, I was a late bloomer in the sense that I hadn't even masturbated by the time Sonny started jerking me off. The act of self-love was so brutally ridiculed and joked about by other boys my age that I dared not do it for fear of being found out. My only ejaculations came in my sleep or when I was "acting" with Sonny, and he and I had never spoken about them. But I'd grown dependent on him for sexual release. Now he'd taken this pleasure to a level higher, one I never would have considered on my own.

When I returned to my room, Sonny was naked upon my bed and fully erect.

He patted the empty spot beside him. "Now you do me."

I was fourteen the night it happened.

Mom and Dad were out on a dinner and movie date and had ordered two pizzas for me, Noah, and Sonny, who was spending the night. By this time our sexual activity had *evolved*. Sonny's passion for "acting" included costumes he made by stealing clothes from his mother and younger sister. The skirts and blouses intensified my attraction to him. I no longer had to close my eyes to imagine he was one of the girls from school.

My favorite item was a pair of his sister's panties. *Pink*.

I'd never known underwear came in pink—and I had a crush on Sonny's sister, even though she was two years younger than me. So we got a lot of use out of those panties. Eventually Sonny gifted them to me, and I kept them under my mattress. If Sonny's sister missed them, she apparently never brought it up.

On this night, Sonny brought me a belated birthday present. He told me to wait outside my bedroom door until he said it was okay to come in. I stood there, anxious and a little nauseated. My homophobia had been germinating into self-hate, and I lived with a constant low-level fear someone would discover what we'd been doing, and I'd be marked as a gay forever. Sonny, meanwhile, was becoming more openly feminine at school and my new friends made fun of him to the point I had to tell him we couldn't be seen in public together. I knew this hurt Sonny, but he accepted it. Having few friends, the kid had little choice but to abide by my new rules. I often told myself I was going to sever ties with him and end this playtime of ours for good, that it was a phase that was behind me. I'd already gone on a few dates with real girls, but lacked the nerve to even kiss them, let alone ask them to jerk me off. For now, as much as I hated admitting it to myself, I still needed Sonny. He'd become a sex toy.

"Come in," he said in his high, fluttery voice.

When I walked inside, my jaw fell. Sweat rose on my brow. My friend stood before me in a pink dress and fluffy petticoat beneath, a little pink bow atop his head. It was the same outfit his little sister had worn at her latest dance recital. I'd seen the picture above the fireplace at his house. The dress was tight on Sonny, as were the bobby socks. He'd brought along the buckle shoes but couldn't fit into them all the way.

I undid my jeans in a hurry—before he could even finish singing Happy Birthday. But just as Sonny took hold of me, I heard my brother crying my name from the living room. I seethed at the interruption.

"Hold on," I told Sonny. "Stay right there."

He was down on his knees before the bed, his face flushed. He didn't budge. I went into the living room where Noah was struggling with the VCR. He could never fully grasp how it worked but always attempted to use it on his own, resulting in these mini tantrums.

"My movie's over," my brother said, hitting every button on the deck.

I was anxious to get back to Sonny. I didn't have time to stand there while *The Never-Ending Story* rewound. I took the tape out of the VCR and looked at the ones Sonny had brought over for tonight's movie marathon, which would start after Noah was put to bed. Sonny's mom had two VCRs and would make copies of every movie they rented. I scanned this latest stack.

The Sixth Sense.

American Beauty.

Sleepy Hollow.

They were all fairly new and I'd seen none of them. *The Sixth Sense* was popular enough that I knew it was a horror movie, so that wouldn't work. I wasn't sure what *American Beauty* was really about, but Sonny had grown obsessed with the young blonde in it and was most excited for me to see it, which I knew meant it contained sex and nudity. So I couldn't show Noah that one either.

I put in *Sleepy Hollow*. It was a live action version by Tim Burton. I knew he'd directed *Batman,* which Noah loved, and I remembered the old Disney version of *The Legend of Sleepy Hollow*, so I figured it would be along those lines. Popping it in, I retrieved a fresh soda for my brother, so he'd have no further reasons to interrupt my playtime.

It wasn't the first time Sonny performed oral sex on me. We'd been doing it for months, with him always the giver and I the receiver. I never so much as touched his penis anymore. It made me feel too much like a queer. I only kept Sonny around to pleasure me, and once he'd brought over a copy of *Hustler* he'd stolen, the "acting" had escalated to blowjobs.

I was in Sonny's mouth when Noah barged in on us. He was already crying for me—the movie having terrified him within minutes. But when he saw what we were doing he actually *screamed.*

I shoved Sonny to the floor. "Stop it, you fuckin' faggot!"

I turned away from Noah, but he'd already seen my erection by the time I put it back into my jeans. Sonny gazed up at me with wet eyes, his lipstick smeared. His bow had fallen off his head. He looked utterly repulsive to me now.

Noah's eyes were wide. "You're being dirty, Jack! You were going tinkle in Sonny's mouth!"

"No, I wasn't, Noah. That's not what happened."

Sonny tried to concur, but I snapped at him. "Shut up!" I came to my brother and took his arms in my hands. "You don't understand, Noah. You're confused."

"Why is he dressed like a doll?" Noah asked.

"Sonny and I were just playing a game."

My brother shook his head, eyes closed tight. "Nu-uh! You were being dirty, Jack. I know you were. You and Sonny both. You're not supposed to do stuff like that!"

"It was a mistake," I said, desperate, frantic. "Sonny did it. I didn't know what he was doing until you came in. I was just about to kick his ass for it!"

Sonny had gotten to his feet. I shoved him back to the floor and reared back and kicked him in the stomach. Now, he and my brother were both crying out.

"Get outta my house, faggot!" I said.

Noah grabbed my shirt. "Don't hit him, Jack! That's bad too!"

Sonny saw his chance to get away from me and took it. He grabbed the backpack with his street clothes in it and tried to push past us for the bathroom. When I reached for him my big brother held me back.

"Stop it, Jack!" he said. "Leave Sonny alone."

Even with the bathroom door closed I could hear Sonny sobbing.

"You better be getting dressed in there!" I said to the door. "I want you outta my house, you fuckin' homo!"

"It's mean to swear and call people names, Jack," Noah said. "It's not all Sonny's fault. You were being bad too."

Now I was the one who wanted the bathroom. I felt on the verge of vomiting.

My older brother was my first experience with a snitch. He never missed an opportunity to show our parents how responsible he was by ratting me out for misbehaving. It got so even my parents told him not to be such a tattletale, but Noah persisted. My mother explained to me that it was his way of being the older brother—that in his mind he thought he was teaching me to do good by telling on me when I was bad. Well, this was as bad as I'd ever been. Noah had caught me with my dick in my friend's mouth while he was dressed in his sister's clothes. The moment my parents came home Noah would tell them everything. My dopey, self-righteous brother would sing louder than Axl Rose.

I continued to try to convince him he hadn't seen what he saw. Noah wasn't having any of it. He was head reporter with the scoop of a lifetime. This was his picture of Bigfoot.

Sonny charged out of the bathroom in his normal boy clothes. I went for his throat but Noah put his arms around my waist and actually picked me up off the ground. Sonny escaped, saying nothing, just weeping like the sissy he was as he left my house for the last time. No matter what happened now, what little remained of our friendship was gone. Our role-playing games were finally over.

"I'm telling," Noah said.

Though I already knew he would, hearing him say it turned the screw deeper into my soul. My hands began to shake. All the moisture left my mouth.

"Noah," I said, lowering my voice. "We have to keep this a secret, okay?"

He shook his head. "Nu-uh. You were bad, Jack."

"I'm serious, Noah. You can't tell anybody about this. I'll be in real big trouble. Huge! Mom and Dad will send me away from you."

His face went slack. "They will? No . . . no, they won't."

"Yes, they will. If people find out what Sonny was doing to me, Sonny and I will both go to jail for the rest of our lives."

My brother gasped. "Jail?"

"That's what they do to bad people. You know that."

"But, Jack—"

"I know, I know. It wasn't my fault. Sonny was the one doing something bad *to me*. But people won't understand that. Not even Mom and Dad. They'll want to punish me forever. I'll be sent away and you'll never see me again. Not ever, Noah."

"No!" Tears flowed down his cheeks. "No, no, no. They won't do that. That's . . . that's not allowed! Moms and dads can't do that. They have to love their kids."

"They won't have a choice. Being this kind of dirty is against the law."

Noah started breathing heavy, the way he always did when he was confused. He tugged on his hair.

"Big bro," I said, taking his hand. "You're my big bro, right?"

He nodded, sniffling.

"Brothers look out for each other," I said, "and big brothers protect their little brothers, don't they?"

He nodded vigorously.

"I need you to be my big protector, Noah. Just like Batman and Spider-Man. Look at me." I raised his chin for him. His eyes met mine. "You don't want me to get hurt do you?"

"No way! I love you, Jack!"

"You don't want me to go to jail and never see you again, right?"

"Nuh-uh. No way! I won't let nobody do that to you, Jack. I swear! You're my little bro and I'm your big bro." He pounded his chest like a gorilla. "I'm here to protect you!"

I pulled him into a hug, and he embraced me with a strength I hadn't realized he possessed. At twenty-one, Noah dwarfed teenage me considerably.

"This has to be our secret, bro," I said. "The biggest secret ever."

"Our big secret. That's right, Jack."

I sighed with relief.

"It's our secret, Jack!" he said again.

"Right. We can only trust each other, Noah."

It was one sentence too many. My brother's big, dumb face went slack and he shook his head.

"No, no, no," he said. "We can trust Mom and Dad, Jack. We can *always* trust Mom and Dad."

The bottomless feeling returned to my stomach. I went through it with Noah all over again. He was enthusiastic about being my protector and assured me, repeatedly, that he'd keep our secret.

But I knew he couldn't.

CHAPTER TWELVE

THE DAY AFTER the story of missing eleven-year-old Seri Davidson hit the news, the press connecting the dots to another recent tragedy further intensified its coverage.

"Channel Six has discovered that the father of the missing girl is Roy Davidson, who was recently charged with manslaughter in the death of twelve-year-old Robert Lucchese. The boy was struck by Davidson's car, an accident in which Davidson had a blood alcohol level of point four—five times the legal limit."

As the newsman rattled off more details, I leaned forward, elbows on my knees as I stared at the television. Natalie was in the bedroom, putting on the new dress I'd surprised her with—one of the "just because" gifts I liked to throw at her. She'd been prepared to make dinner tonight, but I'd stopped her as she'd pulled out the pans, kissed her passionately, and insisted I take her out tonight. She'd been duly wooed.

"Robert Lucchese was the only son of known crime boss Pino Lucchese . . . "

I bit down on the filter of my Camel.

" . . . whose past offenses include loan sharking, racketeering, bribery, assault and . . . "

Natalie said something from the bedroom. Though I heard her words they did not register. My attention never left the screen as they showed old footage of Pino from one of his trials, followed by the same recycled images of Seri, including the blurry picture of her and I together.

" . . . *has left some to speculate the Davidson girl's disappearance could be an act of revenge perpetrated by organized crime . . .* "

This wasn't local news anymore.

We had gone national.

"Honey?" Natalie said, coming up behind me. "Did you hear me?"

I quickly changed the channel. Apparently, *Wheel of Fortune* was still a thing—and so was Pat Sajak. I turned around to see my girlfriend, looking delectable in the tight, navy blue dress.

"What, babe?" I asked.

She leaned over the back of the sofa and slung her arms around me, kissing my ear. "I said I love the dress. You're so sweet to me, Jackie. So thoughtful. You're always full of surprises."

With the exception of forcing my way into her in the kitchen, I hadn't been physically abusive to Natalie for some time. Not only was I keeping my discussion with Giuseppe in mind, but I also had other, richer avenues for my sadism. By now Natalie knew many of the things that would automatically set me off, but I remained purposely inconsistent, which left her moving around me as she were tiptoeing through broken glass—cautious, grateful, and utterly submissive. I'd broken her like a horse. I'd also grown to enjoy having her around—much as I'd enjoyed sharing my cell with my bottom bitch, Ginger. Any home can benefit from a woman's touch . . . as long as she knows what to touch and when.

Natalie returned to the bedroom to finish doing her hair and makeup. I turned the station back to the news. They'd moved on to a story about a celebrity engagement. Polished faces with smiles like rub-on tattoos. Natalie wasn't the type to follow the news, but she was bound to see Pino's face on TV now that these rumors were circulating. Though she didn't know him exactly, she'd been to his house for the barbeque, and he came into the deli to see Giuseppe about business and briskets. Still, I doubted she knew he was a gangster. Since his release from prison, he'd kept a low profile. At least until now.

Natalie knew I was on parole, but thought it was for a simple arrest for marijuana. She also didn't know I worked for Pino. She knew nothing of my meetings at his house. She believed I was an insurance man. But if she started following the story because she recognized Pino, would she recognize the police sketch of the story's mystery man? Was she familiar enough with my body to identify it as the one in the photo spinning the vanished girl at the skating rink? And then would she think of the roller-skates I'd bought for her to wear during sex? Natalie was meek and shy, easily conned if you knew her soft spots, but she wasn't stupid.

As she curled her hair in the bathroom, I snuck to the air vent where I kept those items I didn't want her or Hugh Autry to find. I moved aside Vin's pistol and slid the container of the jewelry I'd stolen and opened the lid. I'd planned to give these items to Natalie for special surprises when she needed them most but, having dished out so little punishment on her lately, I'd felt no need to go diamond-level big with kindnesses. I figured the bracelet could be for Christmas, the earrings Valentine's Day. But things had quickly changed. I had to arm myself with the most fitting arsenal at my disposal.

I took the ring box from the container and closed the vent up.

That night, I got down on one knee at Mama Luna's. The entire restaurant fell into silent awe. The diamond ring gleamed under the soft, amber light, courtesy of the late Gil Yakel. It fit Natalie's finger pretty well, considering, but I would get it resized for her later. The surprise was the important thing. And when the diners cheered and our servers applauded and the violin man came to our table playing "What Are You Doing the Rest of Your Life?", surprise was all I saw on Natalie's face—surprise and a profound love she would never allow to be taken from her.

I dropped by the house the next morning, slightly hung over after celebrating my engagement with my new fiancé. The smell of the McDonald's breakfast in the bag made me nauseous as I drove over, but I was feeling charitable and decided to give Seri her first hot food since she'd been under my care. She raced to the foot of the stairs when I opened the door. As I hit the landing, Seri wrapped her arms around my waist and buried her face into me. In all my life, I doubt anyone else had ever been this excited to see me—not even my parents when I'd first popped out of Mom.

"You were gone so long," she said. "I was worried you weren't coming back."

I patted her head. "Don't be silly."

"Please, don't leave me alone here anymore, Leo. Please . . . I can't . . ."

I made soft shushing sounds as I held her. "It'll all be all right now, love. Don't cry. I'm here for you."

Pushing the bag into her hands, I took up the bucket and did the whole cleaning ritual while Seri ate, sprayed the deodorizer, and did a quick inventory. The bedding would need washing soon. Her pillow was almost as greasy as the McDonald's bag.

"I'm going to draw you a bath today," I said.

She stared at the floor, already ashamed.

"You don't want to be dirty, Seri. It's bad to be dirty."

I stared at her until she nodded in agreement.

"You'll have your privacy," I said. "No peeking on my end. But I'll be right outside the door, so don't try and pull anything."

"I won't, Leo. I promise."

As we came upstairs to the kitchen, Seri squinted against the brash sunlight of the uncovered windows. I walked her to the bathroom hand in hand, just like at the skating rink, and ran the tub. I'd bought a plain bar of Dove and a pink bottle of Mr. Bubble to hide her shame. Leaving the door open just a crack, I sat outside the bathroom with my back to the wall as she undressed. When the tub stopped running, I heard the delicate splash of her hand testing the water, and I closed my eyes and thought of the little boy who'd been using his hand to slurp brown water out of a hole

138

in the earth when the hospital behind him was suddenly bombed, and how me and my fellow soldiers laughed as we watched him be crippled by the blast.

"Leo?" Seri said, her voice echoing through the empty house.

"Yeah?"

Though I couldn't see her face, I could feel her hesitation. When she finally spoke, her courage impressed me.

"What's going to happen to me?" she asked.

Now I was the one to hesitate. I listened as she washed herself—a sound so intimate it made my chest ache with an unidentifiable longing. Seri wasn't crying anymore. Did that mean it was my turn? Those gentle splashing sounds . . . so paralyzing in their innocence and beauty. I felt suddenly deracinated.

"Leo?" she asked.

She said my name as if I might no longer be there, as if I ever was.

"What?" I asked.

"What's going to happen to me?"

I struggled. "I'm not sure."

And it was true.

Pino didn't invite me to his house this time. He wanted to meet the way Vin used to—a desolate location in a parked car. The way Pino probably had done for decades until he got too comfortable.

Well, he wasn't comfortable anymore. He sat beside me in the backseat of the limo, his driver the same heavy he'd brought to my apartment right after the whole fiasco at Gil Yakel's. Pino raised the divider for privacy. His eyes were bloodshot, and he hadn't shaved, something he'd always been diligent about even in the joint. He was dressed down in one of those guinea jogging suits. None of his usual high-class flair. His perspiration smelled of alcohol.

"This is no good, Jackie."

I played dumb. "Something wrong?"

"The girl," he said, scowling. "They're asking me about the girl."

"Cops?"

"Fuck the cops! They've got nothing! I ain't worried about the fuzz, Jackie. I'm worried about D'Arco."

The name chilled me. "Wait . . . you don't mean . . . "

"Who else?"

Angelo D'Arco. A gangster I'd never met but had known about for years. Any criminal in the northeast was wise to follow D'Arco's story but had to be crazy to get involved in it. Working with him, you could end up with thousands of dollars in three separate accounts or your body scattered in three separate rivers. Every story about Angelo concluded with extremes.

"What's he got to do with any of this?" I asked. "He's not your captain or something is he?"

"Fuck no! What am I, an asshole? Angelo's part of the New York City outfit, not ours."

"So what does he care then?"

Pino sighed. "A lot of the old guys have rules about who gets whacked. No women, no children. Seems Angelo considers that one of his ten commandments or something."

"So he's got a grudge against guys who've been naughty. Wants to slap our wrists."

"It's nothing to joke about, Jackie. That goddamned news story broke and now he's got people asking around about the Davidson girl, me, and who the mystery man in the photo is." He poked me. "If he decides I orchestrated a hit, he and his boys will come for us like the four horsemen of the apocalypse."

"You're rather biblical today."

He fingered the pendant around his neck. "This is St. Jude. Know what he's the saint of?"

I shrugged. "Good intentions?"

Pino shook his head. "He's the saint of lost, hopeless causes. Maybe you should get one of these too."

"Don't be so dramatic. The girl's considered missing, not dead. She's just as likely to be a runaway as she is a murder victim."

"Yeah, well, that runaway shit might wash if she were a teenager, but it's a stretch at eleven." Pino crossed his arms, his eyes like ashen jade, searching for something in me. "I know I said I didn't wanna know, but given the circumstances—"

"Pino don't."

"—I need to know what you did with her and where the body is."

"Jesus." I pointed to the divider between the driver and us. "You sure that hired goon of yours can't hear us?"

"Positive. Now what happened to the girl?"

"C'mon, Pino, you know as well as I do it's better you don't know any details."

He leaned into me. "Jackie. I am telling you this

for your own good, not just mine. This is not a situation to take lightly. Angelo D'Arco is not to be taken lightly *at all*. He's the last person on God's green earth you want to take interest in you. We gotta work together on this if we're gonna avoid assassination."

"Assassination?" I scoffed. "You said Angelo has no authority over you and he sure as shit has none over me. He comes for us, it doesn't have to be assassination. It can be war."

"For fuck's sake, we want to avoid that at all costs! The guys in my outfit are already looking at me cockeyed, thinking maybe the news is right, that I had the girl killed. If this starts a war, they might hand me over to Angelo as a peace offering. Maybe even off me themselves. Now listen, if the kid's body is somewhere it can be found, it may be wise to move it. I can see to it that it's pulverized and disintegrated."

"Don't worry. She's at a safe location." I chose my words carefully. "She's underground and will be more trouble to move than it's worth."

"All right. So what did you do to her?"

I returned his hard stare. "What difference does it make? If Angelo's coming, he's coming."

Silence hung between us like static on a dead line. Pino ran his hand over his face, looking old and gray, a broken-backed mule. How much could I trust him now? How much torture could he withstand before giving Angelo's New York crew my name and address? Pino was not a snitch by nature. He'd proven that at his trial and in prison, never giving up names to lessen his own punishment. But there's a difference between keeping your lips sealed when some DA is dangling a carrot and keeping them sealed when someone's taking bolt cutters to your fingers.

"We just have to take every precaution," Pino said.

I gazed out the window. "I will."

CHAPTER THIRTEEN

"**I** NEED A RIFLE."

Max put his empty beer bottle upon the bar. "I figured you'd be strapped already."

Placing beers before us, the bartender wiped moisture from the bar top, but his eyes stayed on me. He was a fit man with natural blonde hair—the eyebrows gave it away—and looked barely old enough to drink alcohol let alone serve it. His limp wrist told me why he'd been staring at me whenever he thought I wasn't looking. Though it was Saturday and The Chimney was packed, the bartender's baby blues kept coming back to me. I figured his skin was like a velvet painting of Elvis, his anus bleached to take beatings like an Everlast bag.

"I've got a piece, yeah," I told Max once the bartender pranced off. "But I need a rifle, a special one."

"You know me, I mostly deal in . . . well, *mind expansion*. I'm a stoner not a fighter. But I might know a guy what could help ya. What do you mean by special rifle?"

"A beast of a Remington. Say a M2010 ESR, something like that."

"Shit, man. I don't even know what the fuck that is."

"It's an enhanced sniper rifle. Not a deer rifle, but a military weapon."

His eyebrows rose. "The fuck you want that for?"

"I'm an American."

"Oh yeah." Max chuckled. "Mass shootings are our national pastime."

"I ain't asking for a dual Uzi here."

"Good. They tend to jam."

"Point is I want a sniper rifle. Something with range and accuracy—not some point-and-spray machine gun. I used this sort of artillery in the service. Let's just say I'm sentimental."

"You've got rose-tinted glasses for a *gun*?"

"Hey, I killed twenty-eight hajjis in the Gulf with a rifle like that. It's kind of like a football star wanting to keep his game ball."

His smiled faded. "Jeez, man. Really? Twenty-eight?"

"Confirmed. There're probably more."

I sucked back the last of my bourbon and Blondie was on it. "Get you another?"

I almost expected him to call me "sugar" or "hon," like some country-fried waitress at a Waffle House. Ordering another belt, I paid cash and gave him a generous tip. If Max noticed the flirtation, it didn't seem to discomfort him.

"I'll see what I can do," he said, "but something like that'll come with a hefty price tag."

Blondie put my drink before me. I made a point to brush my fingers over his as I took it. Max finished his beer and headed to the bathroom.

The bartender leaned on the counter. "What's your name?"

"Jack."

"Mikey."

He offered his hand. It was like squeezing a bag of mashed potatoes.

"What time do you get off, Mikey?"

His fair skin bloomed pink.

Max said he'd call me tomorrow—on my new burner phone—and left after one more beer. I stayed at the bar another hour and forty minutes until Mikey's relief came in so he could take his lunch break. Once out back, I did a line of coke and put another on the back of my hand. Mikey snorted it up with a dollar bill.

"I don't usually do this kind of thing," he said, my hand under his shirt, pinching his nipple.

It was ten at night. No one saw him blow me behind the dumpster. Most of the time, fags give better head because they're men and know what men like, but Mikey was clearly a novice. Maybe he'd only recently come to accept he wanted a dick in his mouth. When I finished, he started undoing his belt. I thought of Sonny Tipton when he'd said "now you do me" after he'd jacked me off for the first time.

I smirked. "You must be joking."

Mikey's face soured. "But I took care of you."

"Whine some more. Fags find that real attractive."

I lit a cigarette and started walking.

Mikey took my hand. "Hey, hold on a second, Jack—"

I pulled him into me and kneed him in the balls. He folded in on himself, gasping in pain.

"That oughta take care of your boner," I said. "Now get lost before I give you the Matt Shepherd treatment, you degenerate cocksucker."

Seri slurped her chocolate shake.

"They were a lot bigger when I was a kid," I said. "Or maybe they just seemed that way 'cause I was smaller."

I'd bought her a new dress, blue and tight. Similar to Natalie's. I'd also wet her hair for her and combed it back. Still, my girl looked faded and dull. Dracula had more color. I preferred fair skin because it showed pink when it was struck, but Seri looked almost sickly.

"You feeling okay?" I asked.

"It's like I'm tired all the time even though all I do is sleep."

"That's depression. Does it run in your family?"

She looked away. "My Dad."

"That why he's a drunk?"

"He is not."

"How do you know he's depressed?"

She went mute. She slurped the milkshake until the cup went dry, leaving only a gurgling echo in its wake. I sat on the cot beside her. She surprised me by not scooting away.

"Did he ever . . . do something?" I asked.

She cloaked herself behind her hair again, so I brushed it behind her ear.

"He did, didn't he?" I said. "All that drunk driving. He didn't care if he lived or died, did he? In fact, he wanted to die."

"No . . ."

"Yes. He was suicidal, wasn't he, Seri?"

When she tried to storm away from me, I grabbed the hem of her dress and pulled her back. She fell into my lap and I wrapped my arms around her, hugging her backwards to my chest so I could whisper in her ear.

"I can see it now," I said. "You going into the bathroom to pee and dear ol' Dad is in a tub full of red water, an old-timey straight razor in one hand and a goodbye letter in the other." Seri's chest heaved with sobs, making me salivate. "What happened? Did he catch your mother doing what she does best with other men?"

"Shut up!"

Again, such a brave girl. It made it more exciting. Was she *trying* to thrill me?

"Or maybe Dad was the one screwing around," I said. "Maybe he was sick of his wife being a fat-assed whale of a whore and his daughter being an annoying little brat."

"Shut up!" She started kicking.

"He wanted out but couldn't escape you two no matter how he tried. So he got loaded and drove around, knocking into trees and little boys."

"Shut up! Shut up! Shut up!"

I held on like a rodeo cowboy as my girl thrashed against my embrace. "Tell me what happened and I'll let you go."

She sobbed. "Please . . . stop it . . . "

"Tell me what *really* happened between your mom and dad and I'll let you go. Tell me about your father's depression and I'll let you out of this basement."

She sniffled. Her breathing slowed as I made tender shushing noises in her ear.

"You . . . you'll really let me go?" she asked.

"Really, Seri."

"Promise?"

"On my brother's grave."

She steadied herself. "My Dad . . . he has a . . . a drinking problem. He tried a hospital for it and did the group with the steps, but . . . " She exhaled. "Dad lost his job. He said he was laid off, but I knew that wasn't true."

"It was his fault."

She nodded. "He was drunk all the time and kept missing work. I heard him and my mom fighting about it. That's when he moved out. Mom didn't want him in the house anymore."

"So he lost his house and family."

Seri's face pinched. A fresh tear fell, and I kissed her cheek to taste it. She went rigid in my arms when my lips touched her flesh.

"Then what happened?" I whispered.

"He . . . he had to go to the hospital."

"Why?"

"'Cause . . . he . . . he had an overdose. On alcohol and medicine. He just mixed them too much."

"Bullshit. He was going for the ultimate escape."

Whimpers. "No . . . "

"There was a sign posted on his problems that read 'no exit'. He overdosed on purpose, Seri. He wanted out of this world and I can't say I blame him. It's a rotten place."

"It wasn't like that."

"Sure it was. And that wasn't the last time he almost offed himself now was it? He kept on drinking and driving, nearly killing himself until he ended up killing someone else."

"It was an accident. He didn't mean to."

"He didn't *care*."

Silence. I allowed her to ease off my lap. She held herself with her back turned to me, not wanting me to see how much I'd pained her.

"Can I go home now?" she finally asked. "Please?"

I took my time lighting a cigarette. The clack of the Zippo was so satisfying. The smoke danced in my lungs like grey dust devils, my mouth fumigated with the savory flavor of slow death.

"Leo?" she asked.

"That picture," I said, pointing to the frame on the desk. "I clipped it from the newspaper, you know. We're stars now, you and me. They even have us on television."

She faced me. "TV?"

"Oh, yeah. Your face is everywhere, a real American idol."

"You mean they're looking for me?" Seri brightened. "I knew Mom would look for me. I knew it."

"Nah, she doesn't care that you're gone, but the police sure do. See, there are laws against a mother neglecting and endangering her own children."

But she wasn't having it. "I wanna go home now, Leo. Please."

"I told you my name's not Leo."

"Well, what is your name?"

I shot smoke from my nostrils, a ghost rider in the sky. I almost told her my name then, just to hear it fall from her mouth. "Maybe I'm the handsome prince, come to wake up Sleeping Beauty."

She had no reply to this. Even I didn't know what the fuck that was supposed to mean.

"What if I were to keep you?" I asked.

Her face fell. "You promised you'd let me go if I told!"

"I'm just speaking hypothetically. Do you know what that means?" She shook her head. "It means just imagine. I keep you, and you grow up with me. I'll be your parent, teacher, and best friend all in one."

More tears and head shaking.

"When you get older," I said, "I can even be your husband. Wouldn't that be nice?"

She went impossibly paler. "No . . . you . . . "

"No? You mean you don't want to wait to get married? Okay, maybe we could do it early. In some states you can marry as young as fourteen or maybe even twelve, long as you have your parents' permission. Those states are down south where people marry their cousins and stuff anyway. Jerry Lee Lewis and all that. I'll have to Google the laws. I'm sure your mother would be happy to sign you away to me. Make it all official."

"I don't wanna marry you."

I stood up, walking slowly toward her. "Don't go breakin' my heart." I gestured to the basement surroundings. "After all I've given you . . . do you not love me?"

She stepped back, her face a prune. I drew closer still.

"Maybe you'll just have to learn to love me," I told her, licking my lips. "Maybe I'll have to teach you how it's done."

Seri darted past, making a dash for the stairs. I just barely got a hold of her before she reached them. She kicked at my crotch, narrowly missing my balls.

So much for karma, I thought, recalling what I'd done to the bartender. I dragged Seri to the cot and shoved her down, looming over her like a drunken stepfather.

"I could do things to you, Seri. Things you'd survive but never recover from. A girl's first time is something she remembers always, even when she doesn't want to—*especially* if she doesn't want to." She squirmed and I pinned her to the mattress. "Boys remember their first time too, *especially* when they're with another boy. You'll never know what it's like to walk around with the word 'faggot' screaming in your own head over and over, but I can make it so the word 'whore' does.

"I can fucking taste your fear, Seri. I can smell your dream of going home. But there's an old saying: *You can't go home again.* Things change while you're away. Perhaps *you* most of all. So when you make your return you find the home you knew is gone." I breathed heavy, feeling the heat flush my neck. "My world is gone, Seri. I don't recognize it anymore. A man spends years in a kinetic desert, killing men, women and children, and then spends more years locked in a cage. When he finally gets out, what kind of world could possibly await him, and what could he possibly bring back with him from his long, dark night in Hell?"

She winced as my cigarette ash fell across her cheeks like snow. "Please . . . "

"Relax. You can take it, girl. We all take it. Take it all our lives."

"No . . . you can't . . . "

"Oh? Why not? What do you mean *I can't*? You calling me a *faggot*?"

Seri snapped. "You said you'd let me go!"

I released my grip and rose from the bed. Seri was raving now, nearly convulsing in hysteria. My threats had driven her deeper into the catacombs of madness than the drugs ever could. Still, I had spiked her new water jug with a fresh sprinkling of PCP. It made for more entertaining home movies.

Seri writhed upon the cot, reminding me of a baby turtle on its back, a bug being cooked by a magnifying glass on a hot day such as this. I wondered if under enough stress someone could be conditioned to have seizures. Maybe I could get a television set down here and play some of those Jap cartoons with the flashing lights and start her on a tailored *A Clockwork Orange* treatment.

"Seri," I said above her cries. "Just remember this—the great thing about dying is you never have to grow old."

I ascended the stairs and bolted the door behind me.

CHAPTER FOURTEEN

NATALIE HAD SEEN the coverage about Pino and the missing girl, as well as the police sketch and skating rink shot. I could tell by the change in her demeanor one night, the way she stayed silent with her eyes on the floor, the sort of behavior I would have rewarded under different circumstances. But she didn't go to the police or pack her bags and hide from me at her parents' house. So while there was suspicion it was clearly smothered by denial. Her fiancé couldn't possibly be involved in such a crime. I was her world now. She had stacks of bridal magazines and had been showing me brochures for tree farms for the ceremony. She wouldn't believe something she didn't want to believe, especially when the evidence wasn't solid.

Still, there was a mild tremor to her tonight. I could see she'd been nibbling her cuticles. As she prepared the chicken parm, I took the bottle of whipped cream from the fridge, snuck up behind her, and tapped her on the shoulder. When she turned, I squirted her in the face with cream, startling and delighting her. I kept spraying as she playfully batted me away. I licked her face, snorting like a piggy. We joked and I caressed her, even helping her prepare the dinner for Christ's sake.

I waited until we'd had some wine before addressing the elephant.

"I saw Pino on the news," I said.

She stopped chewing.

"You remember him, right?" I asked. "Comes into the deli from time to time. We went to his house for The Fourth."

"Yes. I remember. Actually, I saw him on TV too."

"You really think he could've been involved in that poor girl's disappearance? That doesn't seem like him at all."

"I didn't even know he was a criminal."

"Well, *former* criminal."

"Scary either way."

"Maybe so. But I think this is all just prejudice."

She furrowed her brow. "How so, honey?"

"They're only trying to link him to this 'cause he's an ex-con. It's just like singling out a guy 'cause he's black. Pino's served his time. But people will always look at him like he's a gangster, even though he's reformed."

"I didn't realize you knew him so well."

My jaw shifted. "I don't. Not really. Look, maybe he did have something to do with it, but there's no evidence of that. It's all just conspiracy theories. Pino and his family are the real victims here. We know *for a fact* that drunk asshole killed Pino's kid. Nobody knows what happened to the Davidson girl. For all we know she ran off to join a rock band."

"Jackie, she's just a child."

"You're missing my whole point. There's no proof Pino had anything to do with it."

We ate, Natalie mostly just picking at her salad.

"What is it?" I asked.

"Nothing."

"Spit it out, Nat."

She exhaled. "The other man. The one the mother thinks abducted the little girl."

I balled my fists under the table. "The one in that blurry picture."

"Right." She twirled a piece of radish with no intention of bringing it to her mouth. "What do you think about him?"

"Well . . . maybe there's something to that. Or maybe the mom's just a pissed off ex-girlfriend pulling at strings for someone to blame." I sipped my wine as if contemplating. "You know, Nat, most of the time when something bad happens to a child, the crime is traced back to a family member. Maybe the mom killed her daughter and is just making this guy up to take the attention off her."

"Oh, my."

Her face told me she hadn't thought of that, but I certainly had. I enjoyed knowing Seri's parents and other relatives were being thoroughly investigated.

"She could've just invented the guy out of thin air," I said. "A sketch is just a sketch, and it might not even be the girl in that picture. It's so blurry it could be anybody."

Natalie nodded. "That's true. Who knows?"

She started eating again and I relaxed my hands, leaning back into my chair.

"It's just so sad," Natalie said. "Poor little girl. I sure hope she's okay, wherever she is. I hope she isn't with some creep."

A plastic manufacturing plant in Derby that had closed down years ago. Weeds had broken through the cracked parking lot and the front gate was in disrepair, leaving it wide-open for entry. At the back was a smaller, storage warehouse, deep in the shadowy part of the lot where the streetlights didn't shine. I parked and called Max's phone. The building's front doors opened.

Max and a giant black man were standing in front of a pickup truck. Max unlocked the cover on the bed and rolled it back, revealing the transported goods. Cold, blue steel and hard plastic reflected the moonlight that fell through the small holes in the building's dilapidated roof. Four rifles. The bigger man drew one out.

"Remington model 700P," he said. "Mission ready, mission adaptable."

I inspected the weapon. A 5R RACS rifle, built for military and police use with a next-gen chassis system, the shot-to-shot consistency being the best in the industry. This was no standard hunting rifle. The five lands deformed the round less as it sailed through and the angular edges allowed the bullet jacket to more easily form, creating a better gas seal for improved velocity and accuracy. I'd used rifles like this with great success during my years as a killer for Uncle Sam. This rifle came with ammunition and a Tactical Weapons System. I had no need to look at the others. I paid cash, unfazed at the black market markup.

"PCP and now this," Max said with a shit-eating grin. "You're up to somethin', man. And I don't wanna know nothin' about it."

CHAPTER FIFTEEN

DREA LUCCHESE LAY on her belly, stretched out on the lawn chair like a bronze dessert. She'd undone the snap of her bikini top so not to leave a tan line and the smooth skin of her back was a summery beige, her Italian genes responding to the sunshine. One flip-flop dangled off a foot, the other lay upside down on the concrete poolside. Watching her through the scope mounted on the Remington, I felt the sudden urge to shoot her, just for laughs. Nothing fatal, just a round to the spine—something to leave her like Larry Flynt. Imagine how surprised she'd be; how devastated to never even find out why. But she wasn't what I was here for. She only offered a nice view while I waited on the bluff in the woods behind Pino's house. I was low in the tall grass, the rifle mounted on a tripod. I'd worn a camouflaged jumper and applied face paint to cover me under the cloudless August sky. It was good to feel like a meat-eater again. Sweat slicked my back. I needed a cigarette and a drink, and watching Drea's little bottom wiggle in her bathing suit, I wanted to sodomize someone.

How old was she again? Sixteen? Seventeen? Old enough to enjoy it.

I heard the glass door come open and spun the

scope. Rosalie exited the house and walked along the rim of the pool in her floppy garden hat. Now would be an even better time to paralyze Drea with a bullet. Her mother could watch it happen. After losing her son, the horror of it might break her for good.

Pino came out of the house, carrying a cooler and smoking his last cigar. I allowed he and Rosalie to get comfortable on their reclining lawn chairs and, once he was settled with the tanning reflector board in his hands, I centered the crosshairs on his face. It's important to *squeeze* the trigger, not pull or jerk it. A steady squeezing motion, almost sensual in its way.

Pino's neck jerked back as part of his forehead burst.

Blood spattered against Rosalie and she shrieked like nothing I'd ever heard.

Perhaps she would snap for good after all. Drea jolted up so quickly she forgot her top was off and I got a glimpse of her titties. So young and tender. She retrieved her top and ran to her parents, joining in her mother's cries as blood continued to gush from her father's skull. I wondered what kind of flowers the Lucchese women liked and if candy was an acceptable gift for the bereaved. Breaking down my weapon, I paused as a blue butterfly landed upon the very tip of the barrel. There was a bittersweet sadness in that contrast. It left me longing for something I could not name but knew was forever gone.

Melancholy can be so beautiful.

In time, Drea would learn that.

"You been duckin' me, Saul?"

The restaurateur put up his hands. "Nah, Jackie. Just been busy is all."

"Busy pissing away money you don't have again?"

"Nah, Jackie. C'mon, I've got my spending under control now."

I shoved him against the alley's brick wall. Saul was not a big man. It had to hurt. There was something about the restaurateur that made me enjoy knocking him around. He was so sniveling, so willingly defenseless.

"You need to remember your responsibilities," I said. "Now where's this month's payment? Pino don't like late payments."

"I was just about to put an envelope together. I swear on my mother."

"Let's go inside."

I walked him back into the restaurant and we went to his office. Papers everywhere, stacked like pancakes and pinned to the walls. Empty coffee cups decorated the desk and shelving. A frozen clock hung crooked on a nail. I closed the door behind us as Saul unlocked the file cabinet and removed the cash box. He counted out twelve hundred.

"You want an envelope?" he asked.

"Count out the rest first."

He blinked. "What rest? This is what I always pay. Twelve hundred."

"There are late fees."

"Jesus, Jackie. C'mon now—"

I backhanded him, the file cabinet shuddering as he tumbled into it.

"Twenty percent," I said. "Don't test me, Saul."

He sighed, shaking his head as he counted out another two hundred and forty. He put the two stacks together and handed it to me.

"Good," I said. "Now next month's."

"What? You can't be serious!"

I grabbed him by his collar and flung him onto the desk. The computer monitor crashed to the floor, mugs rolling off in different directions. I wanted to shove something up his ass. Maybe a stapler or hole puncher—no pun intended—but there were too many people in the restaurant for that. They'd call the cops when they heard him screaming. Besides, I had more accounts to settle today.

"You make late payments, you gotta start paying in advance," I said.

"Jackie, this'll break me for weeks. You're talkin' a total over twenty-six hundred! I just own a restaurant, man. How am I supposed to make ends meet?"

"I don't care if you have to send your mother out on the street to suck off niggers for nickels. Give me the cash. Now."

He got off the desk sluggishly—as if moving slowly would encourage me to reconsider or offer him some other way out. He pawed through the cash box and handed me a third stack.

"Here's nine hundred and fifty. It's all that's left in here." He titled the box, showing only coins.

"Your wallet."

He drew his wallet from his slacks. Another hundred and twenty.

"That's better," I said. "Pay the rest later. See that? I'm cutting you a little break today 'cause I'm in a good mood. I'm not such a bad guy once you get to know me."

He offered me a sad smile. He had to.

I returned to my car to go see George Glover at his package store. The collections weren't due for five days, but I wanted to gather them before word of Pino's death got out. This way, it all went directly into my pocket.

"This'll make you feel better," I said, placing the needle on the desk.

Seri gazed upon it with distrust. She sweated profusely but was wrapped up in her blanket anyway, her face ghostly and patchy. I don't know how someone who'd been in isolation could've caught a bug, but there was no doubt she'd fallen ill. I'd cleaned the bucket out, tossing the vomit, and returned with the paper bag, placing the cough syrup, lozenges, and aspirin on the desk, and then the syringe I'd prepared upstairs.

"What is it?" she asked.

"It's a vitamin shot."

"Like a flu shot?"

"Yeah. Like that."

I tapped the needle, giving it a little push to expel any air, then sat beside Seri on the cot. Her arm was so pale. It was easy to dig a vein.

"Why is it that color?" she asked. "It looks like iced tea."

"Those are the antibiotics."

"You know how to give shots?"

"Sure. I was a medic for seven years."

Seri glowered, doubting my lie, but didn't resist when I took her arm. Maybe she knew it was pointless to fight, or perhaps she'd finally given up, quitting on life just like her drunken old man. She turned her head away as I punctured her vein, face pinching tight as her blood was flushed with the golden-brown elixir purchased from Max Marino. Once she'd been injected with half of it, I smacked the inside of my elbow. My veins refused to stand. I didn't want to blow my first fix in years, so I took off my t-shirt, tied a knot around my bicep, and shot up the remaining heroin. I'd done my drug test with Hugh Autry just that morning. A half dose would be out of my system in five days or so.

Soon Seri was down on the cot. I lifted her legs, put them in my lap, and leaned against the wall, waiting for the release of pain to come over me in a wave as gentle as a mother's kiss. As euphoria bloomed throughout my body, I ran my fingers over Seri's bare toes over and over again, strumming the soft nubs like guitar strings of flesh. The day's heat was muted here beneath the house. My sweat cooled as it rolled down my body, tingling through the layer of numbness. The silence was broken only by my tinnitus. I wished I'd brought a stereo. It'd been so long since I'd put on music for any reason. I wondered what kind I liked. My mind began to drift and, without thinking about it, I lay down beside Seri, pressed close on the small cot. She nuzzled into me, mumbling something that didn't matter as we went on the nod.

Giuseppe told me there was some paperwork we needed to do to keep my tax records straight, so I went down to the deli after closing time to meet with him like he asked. The sales floor was dark as I came inside, the light of the prep room casting a yellow rectangle across the floor.

"What's with the lights?" I asked.

"Oh, the bills, Jackie. Electric company is asking for the sky these days!"

I saw the shadow come up behind me, but had no time to react before I was cracked on the head. I fell to the floor and was dragged across the tile into the light. Giuseppe backed away as the two men hoisted me up, one grabbing me under my arms, the other hammering my gut with the rod he'd used on my skull.

"So sorry, Jackie," Giuseppe said. "I had no choice."

"Shut up old man!" the bat-swinger said.

I tried to kick him and missed. The bat-swinger ordered his sidekick to hold me tighter and cracked the rod across my knee. Pain exploded from my leg to my asshole.

The bat-swinger was flat-faced and gray-haired, maybe fifty or so. He was bulky, like a guy who'd been into weightlifting as a young man and hadn't lost the muscle, only layered it with some fat. He wore a tight polo shirt, showing off the faded prison tattoos on his forearms.

"So this is the big hit man," the bat-swinger said.

I groaned. Somehow these men knew I'd killed Pino. Had Rosalie or Drea seen me on the bluff? Obviously these wise guys were part of Pino's criminal syndicate—a group I'd kept my distance from. Maybe word had gotten back to them about me taking the early collections and they'd put things together on their own. I could play dumb about that. Tell them I didn't know Pino was dead and was just doing my job. But if they were sure I was the one who'd killed Pino, I was seriously fucked.

"Big tough guy, huh?" the bat-swinger said. "Yeah, maybe when it comes to killin' little girls. Not so tough now, huh?"

He jabbed my ribs, robbing me of air. Pain burned across my chest.

The girl, I realized. *He's here about the girl, not Pino.* But how would he know about my involvement with that?

"Who are you?" I asked.

He got in my face, snarling. "Who am I? I'm Angelo fuckin' D'Arco, ya cocksucka!"

I swallowed hard. "I've heard of you."

"Ain't that nice."

"But I don't know anything about no dead girl."

Angelo looked to his sidekick. "You believe the fuckin' *ugatz* on this prick?" He sucked his teeth and stared at me. "You've been caught, asshole. Don't waste either of our time denying it."

"What makes you think I did this thing?"

"You were fingered. And now that I see you in person, you match the sketch and the picture in the paper."

The only one who could have ratted me out would

have been Pino, but I'd killed him two days ago. Angelo wouldn't have waited to nab me, so it couldn't have been Pino.

"Fingered?" I asked. "By who?"

"You think your friends won't squeal when my boys come around? Your buddy there in the hospital wasn't so keen on the idea of bein' knocked right back into the coma."

Vin.

I hadn't known he'd come out of his coma. He was the only other person who'd been there when Pino ordered the hit on Roy Davidson's daughter. Because he'd been unconscious for so long, I'd written him off as nothing to worry about.

"I've got some friends on the force," Angelo said. "One of 'em asked your friend there a few questions for me—asked real hard, ya get me? Vin's worked with Pino a lotta years. I thought he mighta done the hit, but my cop friend tells me he was very convincing denying it. Vin says he tried to stop you from doing the hit. Good on him. It took some real pressure to get him to talk, I'll give him that. Still, though, he's a rat. I got no respect for that."

I breathed deep. "Listen, Angelo—"

"Oh, it's Angelo now?"

"Mr. D'Arco . . . "

"Don't tell me again you had nothin to do with this, Jackie."

"Please, just hear me out. I can explain everything."

Angelo gave me his best Clint Eastwood stare then looked to his goon. "Let him go but keep a gun on him. This oughta be good."

The large man released me. I itched for the snubnosed revolver I had on me but dared not make a move with the barrel of a pistol at my back. I put up my hands. Angelo watched me, unblinking, a death scowl on his face.

"I didn't kill the girl, Mr. D'Arco. I just kidnapped her."

He smirked. "Yeah, sure. Someone else killed her, right? I figured this would be part of your story."

"No, that's just it. She's not dead. She's very much alive."

Angelo squinted, eyes black as the reaper's. "Bullshit."

"I swear it. Pino ordered me to kill her; that part is true. I pretended to agree to it. I mean, he's my boss. I had to follow orders. But I just couldn't kill a child. It's immoral."

I waited for Angelo to agree. He only stared.

"So instead of killing her," I said, "I kidnapped her. I figured it would buy me some time."

"For what?"

"For people to put it together that Pino was taking out revenge on Roy Davidson for running down his son. I figured Pino's own crew would whack him for taking a hit out on a little girl."

"Somebody certainly did."

I feigned surprise. "Pino's dead?"

"Dead as disco. He oughta consider himself lucky someone else got to him 'fore I could. I'd've made him suffer. I don't care what his rank was with his crew. If they stood behind a kid-killer they'd deserve the war it would start."

There was a dark intensity to the man that assured

me what he was saying was true. A gang war was bad for business, but Angelo seemed like the type to let his anger cloud his better judgment.

"If Pino whacked Roy Davidson," Angelo said, "I'd have no beef. But he went after the kid instead. I don't think I believe you, Jackie. I think you killed that girl."

"She's alive. Honest. You let me go and I'll let her go."

He turned red. "You tellin' me how it's gonna be now?"

"If you kill me, she'll never be found. She'll starve to death. Then you'll be the one to have killed her."

He backhanded me, as I'd anticipated.

"Son of a bitch," he said. "All right, then. Where is she?"

"I won't tell you. You have to let me go. Then I'll release her."

"Fuck that! I'll take a blowtorch to your cock! You'll tell me then!"

"That's not fair. Think about it, Mr. D'Arco. I did the best thing I could in my position. And had I known Pino was dead I would've let the kid go already. You release me and I'll release her. Nobody's gotta get hurt. Everybody wins."

Angelo watched me like some human lie detector. I saw many murders in the lines of his face.

"How do I know you've really got her?" he asked.

"I'll show you." I lowered one hand and pointed to my pocket. "There's a phone in here. I'll reach for it slow."

He allowed it. I drew the phone and awoke the screen. This was not the burner I used for calls. It was a device solely for checking the home movies, my live feed of Seri in the basement. I opened the video and pointed the screen at Angelo. His brow furrowed as he took the phone.

"That's live coverage," I said.

Good thing I'd started leaving the light on for her. Seri sat in the sofa chair with her legs drawn up to her chest, just staring into space. She might have been a corpse but for the turning of her head.

"See?" I said. "She's fine. She has a bed and food and water. The girl hasn't been beaten or violated or anything. And she knows she'll be going home soon."

He looked up at me, anger fading. "Pino crossed the line . . . but okay, maybe you did the best you could in a shitty situation. I had a boss once who pushed me too far. But you still gotta make this right, Jackie."

"Believe me, I want to. I'll release the girl. I'll even drop her off in her own neighborhood. But I need to feel safe doing it, Mr. D'Arco. Nobody goes with me, and you give me your word no harm will come to me afterward. I know you're a man of honor. Your word is all I need."

Angelo ran his hand over his chin, debating. I'd given him all I had—including a little flattery. If I could just get him to let me go, I could figure out what to do next.

"All right, kid," he said. "You have my word. Bring the girl home and you're off the hook. But I'm chargin' ya a fine of ten grand."

"Okay. I can swing that."

"You ain't got a choice. This is the only deal you're gonna get."

I was able to breathe again. "I'm glad we could work this out, Mr. D'Arco."

"Get goin', Jackie. I want that girl home safe and sound. You pull any shit, and I'll take that blowtorch to your fiancé's pussy instead."

I froze. "My fiancé?"

"Yeah," he said, smiling devilishly. "Guess I forgot to mention. Once you left your apartment to come to our little meetin' here, I had one of my guys pay Natalie a little visit. He's with her now." He patted my cheek. "You're not the only one who can pull off a kidnapping, kid. You don't really think I'd just let you go without some kind of retainer, do ya? My word is worth something, but yours ain't worth shit. Now hear me on this, Jackie. That little girl gets home by dawn. Otherwise, my boys and I are gonna get Natalie impregnated and cut her tits off. Understand?"

I nodded, biting my lip.

"I'm keeping this live feed phone," he said. "So I can see what happens."

I nodded again. The only important thing was that I got out of there.

CHAPTER SIXTEEN

ANGELO COULD HAVE been bluffing. I didn't doubt his goon had Natalie, but if he really were old fashioned about not killing women and children, would he really have my fiancé gang-raped and mutilated? Maybe he was only a stickler when it came to children and would torture a woman to death without any guilt or shame. A lot of men are like that. But what kind of morality is it to kill adults but not children? What is the cut off age? Thirteen? Eighteen? Twenty-One? At what point are the ribbons cut and the doors flung open?

Angelo had made a foolish assumption by expecting me to care about Natalie's safety over my own. I didn't necessarily want her to be raped and tortured, but it was a reasonable exchange to avoid getting hurt myself. If I were to come up with some way to rescue her, however, it would have to come later. Right now I had to figure out what to do with Seri Davidson.

I couldn't just let her go. That was ludicrous for a wide variety of reasons. I hadn't fucked or beaten the girl, but I'd subjected her to mental torture and pumped her full of narcotics. She was doped up and sickly all the time now. If Angelo discovered this, I'd be just as dead as if I'd killed her.

AND THE DEVIL CRIED

Beyond that, I simply didn't want to let her go.

Seri was *my* girl. I'd put so much time and effort into our relationship. To even consider releasing her was absurd. The thought of that hippo slut Carmen getting her daughter back made my guts squirm. I'd actually fucked that disgusting woman to get close to Seri. Didn't that level of effort count for something? Had I not earned my most treasured possession? Angelo's crew using Natalie as a bargaining tool was actually quite hilarious. Compared to Seri, Natalie was a total throwaway. I'd much rather see her raped to death than have Seri go home. But while Angelo's threat to her was therefore weak, his threat to me remained troublesome. He wouldn't stop with my fiancé. He'd come looking for me. I needed a plan.

I snorted two lines of coke off my dashboard to get me brainstorming. On my way to the house I stopped at CVS for some eyeshadow, lipstick, hair dye, and a bottle of Pepsi. I got a pizza with extra cheese and bought a bottle of Jack Daniel's. No matter what I did with Seri, this would be our last night in the basement. I figured a farewell celebration was in order. When I arrived at the house I brought the stuff inside, then returned to my car and popped the trunk. The Remington remained there, tucked in its sheath. Hugh Autry never checked my car, only my apartment. Having only used one bullet on Pino, I had plenty of ammo left. I brought my weapon into the house and locked all the doors, just in case. I might have been followed. There might be a way to track the location of the camera using the phone Angelo now had. I didn't think either was true, but it was best to take precautions.

"How's my girl tonight?" I asked as I carried the pie downstairs.

Seri gazed up at me with lost eyes. "Did you bring another vitamin shot?"

I smiled. "Did it make you feel better?"

"Yeah. It was kind of weird but felt really good."

"Eat something first." I opened the lid of the pizza and peeled a slice free. "Extra cheese, just like you like it."

She shook her head, so I bit into the slice myself.

"Leo," she said. "I know that's not your name but, I don't know what to call you."

"Jack," I said. It no longer mattered if she knew. "Call me Jack. That's my name."

"Jack . . . I don't wanna be here anymore."

"You never wanted to be here."

"I know, but . . . I *really* don't want to now. I'm scared down here. I don't like being all alone. Why don't you come more often?"

I tossed the crust into the box, looking at my girl. I knew then she didn't want me to release her any more than I wanted to do so. Who was anyone else to say where she belonged or whom she belonged to?

"Don't worry," I said. "You won't be in here much longer."

Her eyebrows rose. "Really, Jack?"

I loved it when she said my name.

"Really, Seri. Now c'mon. Help me finish this pie."

We went through the pizza together, Seri devouring it. She got hot food so rarely. It was important she appreciate it. As we ate and drank, I imagined Angelo watching us on the live feed with a perplexed expression on his face. I poured us drinks from the Pepsi bottle I'd spiked with bourbon and had Seri raise her glass with me.

"A toast," I said. "To making a new family when your original one sucks."

She didn't repeat it until I told her too.

"*Salute*," I said.

Seri winced when she took a sip. "It tastes funny."

"There's medicine mixed in."

I thought, not for the first time, of jacking off into Seri's food. I had yet to do it. The thought of feeding her my natural protein shakes without her knowing stirred something in me, something warm and vicious. I understood why I hadn't raped her. Sometimes it was just better when they wanted it. That's why I'd taken a shine to Ginger in prison, having grown bored of violating frightened new arrivals. There's still a great deal of pleasure in rape, but slowly breaking someone down until you were their only source of love and protection? *That* was a more rewarding form of assault. I was Seri's only human contact and she'd grown attached to me because of it. She'd opened her soul to me. Her body would be next, given time.

Would she be a chubby teen, taking after her mother's genes? Would she suffer bad acne or crooked teeth? Some other physical flaw brought on by the ravages of puberty? Or would she blossom beautifully, like some baroque painting of an angel? Presently she was only average in appearance, so her young adulthood could go either way.

In the end it didn't make any difference. It was not her looks that mattered, it was what I'd done to her, how I would continue to mold this girl into what I wanted and needed her to be, satisfying something in me no other woman ever could.

They could be a wallflower like Natalie.

Or a slut like Carmen.

Or a tranny like Ginger.

They could be young and gorgeous and submissive.

They could be a supermodel or movie star or high-class stripper.

It didn't matter.

They could never be the woman I'd broken down from age eleven with isolation and drugs until I was all she could see.

Seri wasn't quite there yet, but her progress was astounding. Only once she was completely dependent and wantonly gave me her virginity, then it would finally be time to kill her.

I could watch her trust give way to complete surprise as I wrapped my fingers around her throat, staring her in the eyes as I crossed her over to the other side. And in that poignant moment, ecstasy would fuse with despair. Seri would leave her body as quickly as she had given it to me, and I would be reborn through the act of her death, a child forming not in her belly but in my heart, cradled there as a precious jewel in my most secret of gardens.

"Where am I going?" Seri asked.

That she didn't mention home was an indication of her acceptance she never would go back there.

"Have you always been in Connecticut?" I asked.

"Uh huh."

"Born here?"

"Yeah, in Simsbury."

"Have you visited places outside the state?"

A glimmer of concern in her eyes. "A couple times."

"What place did you like best?"

"I dunno."

"Sure you do."

She shrugged. "Florida, I guess."

I nearly spit up my drink. "Florida? Jesus, why?"

"I like the beaches. And Mom and Dad took me to Disney World."

"Well, I'm not going to that shithole." I leaned back, contemplating. "The Florida Keys, however . . . maybe take a cruise to Bermuda or someplace like that."

Seri hung her head. "Jack . . . I don't wanna leave Connecticut."

"Why not?"

"That . . . that scares me."

"Hey now, everybody's scared to leave where they come from, Seri, but it's an important part of growing up."

But I knew this wasn't her reason for hesitation. It was the idea of leaving *with me* that worried her. She just wasn't ready for that yet.

"Seri, honey . . . I'm the only person you've got. There are some very bad men who want to take you away from me, so *they* can have you. They won't be as nice to you as I have, honey. Believe me."

She still wouldn't raise her head.

"Seri, do you know what rape is?"

Silence, but I knew she understood. I could have given her gruesome details, told her things I'd seen in prison, but figured I'd leave it at this. Let her dream up her own horrors.

"Let's go upstairs," I said. "You can take a bath and I'll give you your vitamin shot. Would you like that?"

She nodded, a girl alone on the moon.

I called the landline in my apartment. It rang several times before Natalie picked up, her voice shaky when she said hello. She sniffled.

"Nat. It's Jackie."

"Oh, thank God . . . Jackie, please, I—"

"How many?" I asked.

"Huh?"

"How many are there?"

She paused. "Three."

So Angelo wasn't bluffing. He and his goons were standing by, counting down the hours before they made a feast of my fiancé. I heard a man's voice in the background but couldn't decipher the words.

"Jackie," Natalie said. "They say you kidnapped that missing girl."

"It's a lie. Those men don't know what they're talking about."

"Jackie, please . . . tell me the truth . . . "

"You think I'm lying to you? At a time like this? Jesus, Nat, I'm going to be your husband. There has to be trust."

"I know, Jackie . . . it's just . . . that sketch and the photo . . . they look like you."

"That's why they think it's me."

"But why?"

"I don't know. Have they hurt you?"

"Not really. Just smacked me around when they first got here."

The male voice said something again, too muffled for me to understand.

"Put Angelo on the phone," I said.

Silence followed by mumbling. Angelo came on the line.

"Where's the girl?" he said. "The sun'll be up soon, Jackie."

"I have her. She's safe."

"Looked that way when yous two had your little dinner. What the fuck was that?"

"She's gotta eat, right? Listen, I changed my mind about bringing her to her house."

"Fuck you! You'd better—"

"It's too dangerous. The cops might be staking it out."

He exhaled. "Fine. Bring her here."

That's exactly what I'd been thinking, but wanted Angelo to think it was his idea.

"Okay," I said, trying to sound reluctant. "An even swap?"

"If you make it in time. Otherwise your girl might become damaged goods."

My girl. It took me a second to realize he meant Natalie and not Seri.

"Don't hurt her," I said, not caring either way but needing Angelo to believe I did. "I'll be there in half an hour."

But I was already right across the street from the apartment complex, watching the window. The first gray glow of dawn was fading in and just one light above the stove was on inside my place, allowing me to see only silhouettes. I couldn't tell who was who. It didn't really matter.

Under the cover of darkness, I'd broken into the abandoned building, a bankrupted Walgreens on the bottom floor and a top floor that had been used for God knows what. Perched on the rooftop, I had a clear view of my apartment's windows, one for each corner facing the street.

I peered through the scope. The shadow of a man pacing. Someone sitting in a chair; perhaps Natalie bound with duct tape. Another man smoking. Still no third man. It was impossible to tell which one was Angelo, so I picked the one pacing and followed him back and forth in my crosshairs, just waiting for him to stand still.

When he did, I started shooting.

The pacing man flew backward as the first window exploded, tossing shattered glass to the street. I pumped out rounds in quick succession, the rifle's warm vibrations reminding me of those abysmal deserts and all the sand people I'd slaughtered, tearing their flimsy homes apart and painting the walls with human gore. The smoking man scrambled and as I fired upon him. The person in the chair jerked and fell backward, taking the chair with them. The smoker got low by the windowsill, hiding. I waited with my scope locked. When his hand appeared over the sill with a .45 automatic, as if to fire blindly, I split it with a single shot. Even with my earplugs in, I could hear him scream from all the way across the street.

I got up, the Remington swinging in my gloved hands, and came to the far end of the rooftop, facing the other window of my apartment. I braced the rifle against my shoulder, rigidly still and at my full height, cocaine intensifying my every sense. The red crescent of the rising sun made a glare on the glass, so I opened fire without a solid target, bursting the windowpane in a brazen assault on whatever living things I could destroy.

I paused. Scanning the apartment through the scope, I saw no movement. I couldn't sit here and wait until I did. Someone was bound to have called the police at this point, so I had to work quickly. Though it pained me to say goodbye to such a fine weapon, I couldn't risk being caught with the rifle, so I chucked it down one of the roof's air vents and ran for the stairs, taking them two at a time. I bounded out the door and into the street, sprinted to my complex, and climbed the stairs, my lungs swelling, sweat dripping. I drew my revolver and clutched it in both hands as I reached my floor. Just before I could exit the stairwell the goon who had held me in the deli charged through the doorway with an automatic in his hand, but I noticed him before he did me and fired twice, capping him in the center of his chest. He collapsed into the railing and tumbled down three steps. I climbed over him and sent a bullet through his face—just to be sure—and reloaded.

I came out of the stairwell. My front door hung open and there was a trail of the goon's blood. No one else was in the hall. Unlike Yakel's neighbor Hannah Johnston, my neighbors were smart enough to stay hunkered down when there was a shootout in progress. There wasn't time to sneak up at the edge of the wall and peek inside. A surprise attack was best—much like when we'd ram our way into some hajji safehouse and bomb them with flash grenades so they'd be blind when we stormed in to annihilate them.

I aimed the revolver as I stepped inside. A man was facedown in a pool of blood. The back of his head was concaved by an exit wound in a cavern of red meat, looking almost vaginal. I came around the edge of the counter and saw Natalie on the floor, tied to the overturned chair. If not for her hair, she would have been hard to recognize covered in all that blood. My rapid rifle fire had punched several holes in her, but she was still breathing. She gazed up at me with half-closed eyes and when she tried to speak blood bubbles popped upon her lips. I stepped over her, looking for Angelo.

A trail of blood ran from the side window to the bedroom. The door was closed. I fired two shots through it as I approached, then ducked behind the wall, waiting for return fire. Several shots splintered the door and drywall. I spun and returned fire. The center of the door was all but obliterated and I caught a glimpse of Angelo sitting on the bed, his bloody hand in his lap. It was he who I'd shot through the window, blowing his gun from his grip. Now he had to use his non-dominate hand to shoot.

I fired again to cover myself as I barged into the bedroom. Angelo retaliated but both of us missed. He moved but I was younger, faster, and unwounded. I shot the arm he held the automatic with and, as it dropped from his hand, I straddled him on the bed. This horse was lame now and couldn't ride anymore. I jammed the barrel of my pistol under his chin.

Though in a hurry, I couldn't resist saying a few words, seeing as he'd fucked everything up for me.

"I'm gonna murder that little girl," I told him.

Angelo grimaced. "You son of a bitch . . . "

"It's only fair, considering all you've put me through."

"I was never gonna hurt your girlfriend. Never."

"No need now. I did it for you."

His grimace gave way to shock. "You're a monster. You're a—"

I fired through his jaw, the bullet coming out the top of his skull in a red spurt. Angelo dropped and sprawled out on my bed sheets, drenching them with blood and urine. I went to the airduct and pulled off the cover, pocketing Vin's .22 and the bracelet and earrings from Yakel's vault. I gathered the close to fifteen grand I'd collected in early payments from Pino's accounts, stuffing all my pockets, and crossed back through the kitchen on my way out.

Natalie moaned my name. I'd already forgotten she was still alive. I cursed under my breath and came to her.

"Tough break, Nat," I said with a shrug.

I opened the chamber of my .38, expelled the empty casings, checking how many live rounds I had left in it.

One.

Perfection.

"J-J-Jackie . . . " Natalie whimpered. The wounds in her chest made sucking sounds when she spoke, her lungs flooding with blood. "Jackie, I'm . . . I'm . . . "

I put the business end of my revolver to my fiancé's temple.

She whispered. "I'm pregnant, Jackie . . . "

Natalie moaned, a drop of blood flowing from her mouth across her cheek. She clutched at her belly, mutilated by multiple rounds, and raised her head to look at it, as if she could see the surely dead fetus within.

Sirens wailed in the street, drawing closer.

"I love you . . . " Natalie said.

I shook my head. "I never loved you."

Then I shot her.

CHAPTER SEVENTEEN

I'D PARKED THE Charger behind the abandoned Walgreen's. By now there were shocked spectators on the sidewalk, so I plucked nose hairs to bring tears to my eyes before crossing the street. I peeled out of the parking lot, swerving down back roads, and forced myself to ease off the gas so not to draw attention to myself. A police car raced by, lights blazing crimson against the muted indigo of dawn.

Judging from the chorus of sirens in the streets, the cruiser was one of many.

A fire engine blared. An ambulance wailed.

But it was all behind me now.

That I would instantly become the main suspect in the shooting was inevitable. I was the former military sniper ex-con who lived there. Hugh Autry would probably get a thrill out of aiding in a manhunt, stepping out of his parole officer booties and borrowing real police shoes. He wouldn't be the only one embracing a new role.

Before leaving the house, I'd used my burner phone's camera to take headshots of Seri. She was fresh from her bath and I'd trimmed her hair, dyed it red, and blown it dry. She'd been stoned enough not to fuss with me about it. I'd also put lipstick and eyeshadow on her in an attempt to make her look older. I'd then dyed my hair blonde and shaved it short and had her take pictures of me, using the white walls as backdrop. I gave her a slightly larger dose of heroin than the night before and placed her back on her cot. Always the night owl, Max Marino was awake when I called him.

"Yeah," he told me when I asked for the goods. "It'll cost ya, though."

"Money's not an issue."

"Listen, I've seen the guy's stuff. It's worth it."

Getting on highway 91 now, I headed north, the stacks of cash on the passenger seat weighed down by the two loaded guns. The sun rose in full, giving all of creation its color, lush with the end of summer. It was coming up on Labor Day weekend. I'd realized that while trying to book a place.

I drove for an hour and half, stopping in Massachusetts for a Dunkin Donuts breakfast and a shit before getting back on the highway. The brutal heat had cooled and I drove with the windows down. It reminded me of my youth. All that was missing were Nick and Tina, my old stoner friends, and some rock on the radio—maybe Korn, Rob Zombie, or Coal Chamber, or another one of those dumbass bands that were popular at the time. I turned on the radio. The Door's "Roadhouse Blues." Good enough. My father had liked '60s rock and Jim Morrison's voice always returned me to childhood barbeques and road trips, my brother Noah clapping along but always off beat.

Thinking of him now, I remembered the dipshit look on his face when I'd put all my strength into shoving him into the railing. He'd broken through the wooden poles, not even screaming, just staring at me with those raccoon eyes of his as he fell from the second floor and down into the den, hitting his head on the coffee table and breaking his neck. I just knew he couldn't be trusted to keep his mouth shut about what Sonny and I had been doing that night, so I'd lured him upstairs and told him to lean over the awning and count to ten, which he'd done without asking why, expecting hide and seek. I can't say if I intended to kill him or just thought I might knock his memory clean. All I'd truly felt was rage.

I ran down the stairs to check his pulse—one of the skills I'd picked up in the Boy Scouts of America—but there was no need. His neck bone was actually protruding through his throat. The gruesome sight was disturbing enough to make me cry, so the 911 call sounded all the better.

"My brother fell!" I said. "Please, you've gotta help me!"

No one questioned the incident, not even my parents. Noah was an imbecile and a klutz. He fell all the time, once even breaking his arm. He knocked over lamps and had broken several dishes. Though tragic, there was nothing surprising about his death.

The only one who might have found it suspicious was Sonny Tipton. He'd been at the house just hours before it happened, and my brother and I had been arguing at the time. I covered this by calling Sonny and apologizing for what had happened between us, begging him to forgive me and using my brother's death to milk his sympathy. I made a deep effort to confide in him with my forced grief, sobbing on his shoulder and retelling the tragic scenario I'd made up. I used reverse psychology, even though I didn't know that's what it was at the time, telling him I blamed myself for my brother's death so Sonny could assure me it wasn't my fault. Once I was confident his pity had washed away any potential suspicion, I rewarded Sonny by kissing him for the first time, sealing the deal.

I spent the next month and a half being affectionate with him in private, without it being us "acting." Though I forbade him from being romantic with me in public, I did allow him to be seen with me again. I even went with him to the movies.

One night we were alone in my house, my parents having gone to their weekly counseling meeting—a sort of alcoholics anonymous for people who had outlived their children. That night I fucked Sonny in the ass for the first time. I'd only had oral sex before, so this new feeling exhilarated me. We took it slow, mainly because it hurt Sonny to have his butt cherry popped, but he mistook this slowness for passion and his heart was my prisoner fully and completely. When I felt it was safe to do so, I broke up with him, easing him down gently so he'd not want to retaliate. I told him I loved him but just needed some space to be with my family and time to think hard about whether or not I was gay. Considering the other option was killing him, Sonny got off easy.

After Noah died, I took his photo ID. Unfortunately he had no driver's license. My brother and I looked alike, but I was still just fourteen. I knew it would get taken away if I tried to use it too soon. So I'd waited until I was sixteen before using it to buy cigarettes, and a few years later used it to buy beer and gamble in the Indian casinos. That card was my golden ticket. It was my first fake ID. It wouldn't be my last.

I reached the diner just after ten. The early birds were full and gone but there were still a decent amount of people wolfing down flapjacks and guzzling coffee refills. It looked a hell of a lot better than Dunkin Donuts and made me wish I'd waited to eat.

I was just on the border of New Hampshire now. If not for the excitement I would have been exhausted. It was probably best to hold off on sleep until this was all finished, because the beating I'd taken from Angelo's rod would ache all the deeper once I had slept. Better to be as agile as possible until I reached my destination. Anything could happen. In my experience, it usually does.

Max was right about the guy. I knew he was the connection the moment he walked into the diner. His head was shaved clean, one side peppered with razor rash. Sleeves of tattoos decorated his arms and red suspenders held up his black jeans. Real inconspicuous. Having seen me in the pictures I'd texted to Max, the man recognized me and slid into the booth, a wry smile on his face.

"How're you today, John?" he said.

"It's Jack."

"Not anymore."

He moved his arm under the table. Something brushed my leg. An envelope. I took it and handed him the envelope I'd prepared for him, stuffed with cash. He put it in his pocket without counting it. Maybe he knew how to be conspicuous after all.

"The girl looks a little familiar," he said, smirking. "She a movie star? Think I saw her on TV."

I said nothing.

"No need to worry 'bout me, friend," he said. "I'm not one to judge. After all, I've got a few like her myself."

A log cabin off Spofford Lake. I'd booked it ahead of time, using my newly purchased alias. Max had been right about the quality of the phony driver's license and credit card. The high price tag was justified for work done this well and this quick. Clearly the skinhead and whatever forgery artists he employed were serious professionals. The property manager kept my credit card on file for any potential incidentals, but I paid him in cash up front.

He handed me the key to the most private—and therefore most expensive—cabin on this beatific piece of land. It was on the edge of the lake with a private dock and pier, a canoe and poles to hold fishing rods. The cabin was shrouded in towering, vibrant maple trees and lined by rose bushes, colors bright as fireworks. I backed the car into the driveway and looked around. The seclusion put me at ease as I walked the path to the lake. It glimmered like stars in the late summer sunshine. There was a distant sailboat; otherwise, no sign of human life.

I returned to the car and popped the trunk to let

Seri out. I took the gag out of her mouth, undid the zip-ties at her wrists and ankles, and guided her out, her arms around my neck. She was still dozing from the heroin I'd pumped her full of and it made her docile and agreeable. I carried her into the cabin and placed her on the sofa. She moaned and mumbled as she curled up with a pillow. There was a dartboard and pool table in the den and a mini pool in a glassed-in back patio. The bedroom had a heart-shaped whirlpool tub. Queen bed. Mounted TV on the wall. I gathered our bags and groceries from the car, brought them inside, and locked the door behind me. I took off my shoes. Sitting beside Seri on the couch, I put her head in my lap and ran my hand through her hair. We stayed that way for some time.

I jerked awake, catching myself snoozing. Seri hadn't moved. I slid out from under her and went to the window, paranoid someone could have tailed us, even though I knew it was impossible. I poured myself a belt of bourbon, holding it in my mouth to savor the burn in the back of my throat, so sharp and bitter and serene. I laid out a rail of coke on the counter and snorted it, then lit a cigarette and played with the lid of my Zippo, snapping it back and forth as I watched the trees sway in the mellow breeze. A feeling of calm settled into me. The morning had been chaos, but the afternoon was benign, a moment treasured even as it happened.

I looked over the forged passports again. Jonathan Wallace and his fifteen-year-old daughter, Hailey. I considered taking her to Canada to make police pursuit more difficult, but autumn was coming and I didn't want to face winter in the great white north. The desert had made me accustomed to warmer climates. I fucking hated snow. This cabin was just a temporary hideout. Seri and I could spend more quality time together now. As long as I kept her close, I could prevent her from running. At night I would tie her to the bedpost—at least until I was satisfied we'd established a trust.

Seri stirred and rose from the couch. She looked around, bleary eyed.

"What do you think?" I asked, gesturing to our abode.

"Where are we?"

"In a fairytale. Sorry again for having to put you in the trunk, but it was for your own safety."

She sat up, rubbing her arms. "I heard gunshots. Lots of gunshots."

"I told you—they're after us. I barely got us out of there alive."

"Who are they?"

"An international cult of child killers. They wanted me to sell you to them to rape and torture. When I refused, it got violent."

I couldn't tell if Seri bought it or not. In time, I felt confident that I—along with enough mind-bending drugs—could instill in her the sort of paranoid delusions that would bind her to me. Stockholm Syndrome would take care of the rest. She would become Hailey Wallace. I would be the only one she could trust—her protector and guide in an alternate reality of our own creation.

"Did people die?" she asked, her voice shaky.

"I'm a solider, Seri. Eight years in the United States military. We're just like police officers in that we only use our weapons when we have to. I had no other choice. I had to keep them from getting to you."

"So . . . what happens now?"

"Many of them are still out there. We have to hunker down here for a while and hide to stay safe. They have agents everywhere. It's important not to trust anyone except each other."

She looked at the floor, unreadable. I went to her.

"I'm serious, Seri. We left the house because it wasn't safe there anymore. They've probably burned it to the ground by now." I gently took her by an arm lined with purpled track marks. "C'mon, I'll show you the rest of the cabin. Wait 'till you see the tub."

At the doorway I gave her a little pat on the butt, just to gauge her reaction. She didn't flinch, only entered the bedroom, silent as a ghost. Her meekness excited me. Something in her had resigned.

"How 'bout that heart-shaped tub, huh?" I asked. "It has jets and bubbles and the whole thing. Pretty great, huh?"

Seri didn't respond. I ran one finger down her cheek, the flesh as tender as a baby's belly. When I leaned in and smelled her hair she did not shudder or pull away. I started rubbing her shoulders, bending down so I could whisper in her ear.

"The tub is even big enough for two."

I felt a slight shiver come over her and her shoulder muscles tightened in my grip. She would have to learn to accept physical touch, if not enjoy it. There was still much teaching to do. It was just like training a new puppy—treat or no treat, punishment and reward.

"I want you to relax, Seri. We're safe here for now.

What can I get for you? Maybe a little snack? I've brought candy and popcorn and soda." I kissed her temple. "What can I get for my girl? Just name it."

Finally she spoke. "I want a vitamin shot."

I straightened. "You just had one this morning."

"You said I could have what I wanted."

The habit was slowly becoming an addiction, one more thing that would give me power over her, and perhaps deter her from wanting to leave me. Soon the only escape she would want would be the golden euphoria that released her from dope sickness. Already heroin was becoming her solitary salvation. Rarely did she ask for anything else.

"All right," I said. "But I want you to do something nice for me in return."

She paused. "What?"

"I can't tell you what it should be. You need to decide that for yourself. After all I've given you, how do you want to show your appreciation?"

She pursed her lips and I resisted the urge to put my finger in her mouth. I wanted her to come up with her own idea. She was silent, but I didn't mind if she took her time, so I went to my suitcase and retrieved the kit. I spooned the powder and flicked the Zippo. It was the first time Seri had seen it prepared. She watched as the needle siphoned the fluid from the cotton, more than enough for both of us to get high, so it would already be ready for later. I tapped it with my finger.

"Liquid gold," I said.

"Can I have it now? Please, Jack? I really need it."

I didn't have to ask her to do anything for me. I could simply tell her. She'd bend to my every whim.

A junkie always does. But I wasn't going to utilize this power yet.

"Sit down," I told her.

She went to the bed. I sat beside her and tied the little, rubber hose around her bicep.

"Can you show me how to do it?" she asked.

I looked into those desperate eyes, so gray and faded. Lips chapped. Nose pink, as if it were the dead of winter instead of early September. She was dressed down in jean shorts one size too big and a tight, blue t-shirt.

I saw my opening.

"Your doll dress," I said. "It's in the suitcase I packed for you."

It took her a few seconds to catch my drift. Once she did, she got up and took out the dress, stockings, and even the buckle shoes. She headed toward the bathroom door.

"No need to go in there," I said.

She stared at the floor, her face flushing the same color as the dress.

"We have to learn to be completely comfortable with one another," I said.

Biting her lip, she found the courage to look me in the eye. I was proud of her. Her gaze fell upon the syringe in my hand. It was pointing at her like the barrel of a rifle, waiting to shoot her up. A single drop glistened at its end, catching the sliver of sunlight that peeked through the gap in the curtains, the only light in the brown shadows of the room.

Seri started with the sneakers, then pulled her shirt over her head. She had no need for a training bra yet, but her shoulders hunched, her chest caving in to hide her nudity. The shorts came down, revealing the pink panties with watermelons on them. As she lifted the dress, I almost told her to change panties in front of me, too, just to extend my power, but felt it would be too much too soon. Once she was fully dressed, I patted the mattress and she sat down beside me. I touched her thigh, feeling the stockings' material. It made buzzing sounds as my nails dragged along it.

"That's my good girl," I said.

She actually smiled. She'd obviously feared something worse was going to happen, and now relief and the anticipation of junk in her veins made her warm up to me again. We'd taken another big step in convincing her to love me.

"So, can I do it myself?" she asked again.

I had her sit on my lap, her little buckle shoes dangling. I draped my arm over hers to guide her, and gently placed the syringe in her hand.

"Okay, what you need to do is—"

I didn't get to finish.

The needle went through my right eye, blinding me, the heroin dispelling into my skull. Seri screamed as she stabbed me with it, pushing the plunger all the way down. She was up off my lap before I could grab her. I rose from the bed, doing my best to ignore the pain, and chased her as she fled through the cabin and out the front door. The needle bobbed in my socket as I sprinted across the grass, little bumblebees fluttering about Seri as she charged down the path, screaming for help. We were deep in the woods, but the path led to the other cabins. A mile on, someone might hear.

The little bitch was fast. All that roller-skating had

given her powerful legs. But my legs were longer, and I was fueled by rage. It was time to hurt her. Still only in my socks, my heels ached upon the pebbled path, but still I charged forward, as if I were about to score a game-winning touchdown. But as I came closer to Seri my head began to ache. A profound dizziness overtook me, the vision in my one good eye blanketed by fuzz. But I could still make out the pink form of a girl as she dodged my attempt to grab her by darting off the path and through the small grove of maples. I chased her down toward the lake where she shouted at the sailboat, jumping up and down, arms waving.

Running down the incline, I projectile vomited and fell to my knees. The intraorbital heroin injection was taking effect. A massive dose meant for rationing between Seri and myself, the dope was more than my body could handle. My flesh grew warm and itchy. As I tried to spit the taste of vomit from my mouth, it suddenly lost all moisture. My lungs burned. Placing both hands on the ground, I desperately gasped for air I simply couldn't collect. I clutched my chest. My arms gave out, so I went on my side in the green grass, letting the bees and butterflies sail around me in little halos as I struggled to breathe.

With my remaining eye I could see my precious pink girl hopping along the shore, surrounded by the glitter of the rippling lake.

Summer was coming to an end. Soon dusk would arrive earlier and earlier, bringing darkness and ice, but in this moment the sun was shining down upon my living doll, and she was even more beautiful than when I'd first took her in my arms at the skating rink and spun her in the air against a rainbow of disco lights.

I couldn't breathe at all now.

I had just enough time to see the sailboat turn toward Seri as she cried out from the bank. Then that cold came—the cold and the darkness—and the only peace I would ever know.

ACKNOWLEDGEMENTS

Appreciations to everyone at Stygian Sky Media for the great effort they put into making this book. Thanks to Jarod Barbee for the hard work and good faith. Big thanks to my own personal cheerleader Sadie Hartman for all the wonderful things she does. Thank you to Alex McVey for the exceptional pulp cover art.

Thumbs up to my awesome and supportive friends John Wayne Comunale, Brian Keene, Wesley Southard, Tangie Silva, Ryan Harding, CV Hunt, Josh Doherty, Bryan Smith, Wile E. Young, and whoever I forgot. And, of course, thanks to Bear.

Big thanks to Tom Mumme—always.

ABOUT THE AUTHOR

Kristopher Triana the author of fourteen books, many of which have been translated to other languages. His novel *Gone to See the River Man* made the preliminary ballot for the Bram Stoker Award in 2021 and *Full Brutal* won the 2019 Splatterpunk Award for Best Novel. His short fiction has appeared in numerous anthologies and magazines, and he is the co-host of the podcast *Vital Social Issues 'N Stuff with Kris and John Wayne*.

He lives in New England.

Made in the USA
Las Vegas, NV
11 May 2022

48774674R00122